Simply Beautiful

A NOVEL

P. O. Dixon

Simply Beautiful

Copyright © 2023 by P. O. Dixon

All rights reserved.

No part of this book may be reproduced in any form or by any electronic or mechanical means, including information storage and retrieval systems, without written permission from the author, except for the use of brief quotations in a book review.

This book is a work of fiction. The characters depicted in this book are fictitious or are used fictitiously. Any resemblance to actual events, locales, or persons, living or dead, is entirely coincidental.

Dedication

In heartfelt appreciation to all the devoted readers who inspire me with their unwavering enthusiasm and yearning for more of my stories.

Contents

Acknowledgments	vii
Prologue	1
Chapter 1 - Intentions	7
Chapter 2 - Intervention	15
Chapter 3 - Apprehension	25
Chapter 4 - Confusion	33
Chapter 5 - Communication	45
Chapter 6 - Champion	57
Chapter 7 - Machinations	63
Chapter 8 - Conversation	79
Chapter 9 - Desperation	91
Chapter 10 - Resignation	103
Chapter 11 - Expectation	109
Chapter 12 - Deception	119
Chapter 13 - Separation	125
Chapter 14 - Exploration	139
Chapter 15 - Observation	145
Chapter 16 - Relations	153
Chapter 17 - Connection	167
Chapter 18 - Exasperation	175
Chapter 19 - Consideration	185
Chapter 20 - Confrontation	191
Chapter 21 - Aspiration	201
Chapter 22 - Anticipation	207
Chapter 23 - Assignation	219
Chapter 24 - Reservations	225
Chapter 25 - Reflection	231

Chapter 26 - Explanation	245
Chapter 27 - Consolation	253
Chapter 28 - Determination	261
Chapter 29 - Consternation	269
Chapter 30 - Contemplation	277
Chapter 31 - Confession	283
Epilogue	295
Also by P. O. Dixon	301
About the Author	305
Connect with the Author	307

Acknowledgments

My profound admiration for Miss Jane Austen is immeasurable. She created an incomparable masterpiece in *Pride and Prejudice*—a timeless classic that has continued to captivate readers for centuries.

It is because of her inspiring work that I'm able to craft engaging variations of Darcy and Elizabeth's story and share them with readers around the world. And for that, I could not be more grateful.

"Think only of the past as its remembrance gives you pleasure."

—*Jane Austen*

Prologue

Mr. Thomas Bennet raked his fingers through his hair, and a dark strand fell onto his brow. He caught it with his other hand and pushed it back into place. His gaze rested on his child—a little eight-year-old girl who held her hands to her mouth as she cried. Tears streamed down her angelic face, leaving tiny streaks along her skin. Her anguished sobs filled the air.

"Mama! Mama! Jane!"

The sound of his child crying ate away at Mr. Bennet's heart, but the reason behind her tears caused him the most pain. A young man in the prime of his life, the distraught gentleman now called himself a widower and a single father of a motherless child. His wife, the late Mrs. Francis

Bennet née Gardiner, and his firstborn child, Jane, had perished in a carriage accident a little more than a fortnight ago.

Such pain, unlike anything he had ever known, filled his world. Bennet had never suffered a large family. An only child, he lost his parents to a carriage accident over a decade prior. He had steeled himself against the ensuing pain as best he could, for that was what everyone expected of him. Though his sadness was insurmountable, he had held back his tears with great fervor because that was what grown men did: they did not cry.

A world without his parents had come upon him in an instant. Yet, it was not enough time for him to truly grieve their loss, for, despite Bennet's carefree ways, he had been thrust into a position of power as master of Longbourn Village in Hertfordshire, where people depended on him for their livelihoods.

A sense of guilt had also compounded his suppressed grief—guilt that he had not taken his role as the future master of Longbourn more seriously when he should have by learning what he needed to know from his father. Guilt that he, therefore, had disappointed his father by choosing the gaieties of youth and caprice over the responsibilities of an only son and future heir.

Faced with the daunting task of managing an estate, another more life-altering challenge awaited him mere months after his parents' deaths—a forced marriage to a young woman from the nearby town of Meryton who was with child. Although she was respectable enough, she was by no means the woman his parents would have chosen for him, owing to her family's roots in trade. Her father was an attorney, and her mother was the daughter of an attorney, too, from a neighboring county.

Miss Gardiner was a great beauty, however. What did lineage have to do with anything when the prospect of courting a beautiful woman was at stake for a young man sowing his wild oats? It was the only way he could describe his fascination with Miss Gardiner, for she was not an intelligent woman—not by anyone's standards. In contrast, he was a man of sense and education, a Cambridge man who walked among the pillars of society's elites. How great his love was for her was hard to say and, indeed, wholly irrelevant. His actions charted his life's choice from almost the moment he first danced with her.

"Mama! Mama! Jane!" the child cried out once more.

Mr. Bennet stroked his daughter's soft cheek and wiped away a tear with his thumb. "Hush ... do not cry, my darling child. My little angel is sad because Mama is not here to tuck you into bed and your dearest Jane is not here to snuggle next to you. They are both at rest, though they are surely smiling at you as we speak and are proud of you. I am proud of you, too, for being so strong."

Mr. Bennet then leaned over and kissed his daughter's forehead.

"But I do not want to be strong. I want my mama and Jane," the little girl replied.

"Yes, I know, my dear. I know."

Her small nose crinkled as she sniffled. "Will you stay with me tonight, Papa?"

"If that is what you want, my little angel." Mr. Bennet took off his coat and sat on the bed beside his daughter.

She threw herself into her father's arms and clung to him. "Promise you won't leave me too."

A sharp pang tugged at Bennet's heartstrings as he softly stroked her tiny hand until her eyelids grew heavy and she drifted into a peaceful sleep. He stroked her hair gently until he was sure she was sleeping soundly then leaned over. He kissed her on the forehead, whispered that he loved her more than anything in the world, and left the room with a heavy heart.

No, Thomas Bennet had not cried when he lost his beloved parents in a carriage accident more than a decade ago. He did not cry when he lost his young wife and firstborn child. Though he had successfully held back the tears for so long, the well of sorrow had not been deep enough to contain his grief. As the carriage pulled away from Pemberley Manor in the early pre-dawn hours with the recently widowed young man its sole passenger, all he could do was cry.

Chapter 1 - Intentions

PEMBERLEY IN DERBYSHIRE, 1811

Elizabeth remained oblivious to the fact that her father, Mr. Thomas Bennet, had arranged a surprise visit to Pemberley. Similarly, Fitzwilliam Darcy was unaware of this impending arrival as no one had informed him about it. Given their understanding of the profound bond between Elizabeth and Fitzwilliam, Mr. Gerald Darcy and his wife, Lady Anne, could not help but question their son's capability to keep this visit a secret from Elizabeth.

Mr. Bennet had insisted that his imminent visit be kept secret in case unforeseen circumstances prevented his arrival. Even if he had not, Mr. and Mrs. Darcy would have had it no other way. Thomas Bennet was not known for keeping his word.

Every time he deemed himself fit to see his only child, he wrote to the Darcys, telling them of his wish to pay his daughter a visit. On each occasion when the visit was arranged, he would withdraw at the last minute, citing one excuse after another. Only he knew what the actual explanation was. Others might speculate. Be it his overindulgence in drink, be it gambling. There were quite a few vices from which one might choose.

Indeed, any of those factors could have played a role. Still, the underlying catalyst was always his profound grief, which continued to engulf him a decade later. The haunting image of the carriage hurtling down the cliff, with his wife and elder child trapped inside, remained etched in his mind. Amid the carriage's descent, he had managed to save his youngest daughter, who sat beside him, by clutching her tightly and holding on as they both tumbled from the vehicle.

Aside from Elizabeth and him, there were no survivors: not his wife, elder child, or the drivers. To that day, gunshots rattled him, recalling the instant the horses were relieved of their suffering at his hands.

The Darcys were gathered in the smartly appointed drawing room upon the arrival of Mr. Bennet. Mr. Gerald Darcy, a refined gentleman of distinguished stature, sat with an air of quiet dignity, engaged in polite conversation with his wife, Lady Anne. The room exuded an atmosphere of elegance, reflecting the refined tastes of its occupants.

Fitzwilliam Darcy, their son and heir to the grand estate, stood by the window, his tall and commanding figure casting an imposing shadow. With a brooding air, he stared out at the expanse of lush green lawn below, his thoughts veiled behind a mask of stoicism. The play of sunlight upon his face emphasized the strong angles of his features and the sharpness of his countenance. His expression was guarded, revealing little of the thoughts that swirled within.

Unlike his father, who greeted the guest with all the warmth that could be expected of two long-standing friends, Fitzwilliam barely uttered more than a monosyllable, leaving Mr. Bennet to suspect that the young man harbored some sort of ill will toward him.

If such indeed were the case, he could not blame him. No one was more disappointed in Mr. Bennet than he was in himself. If the parents felt the same as the son, they did not show it. On the contrary, they were as gracious and kind to him as they ever had been, further bolstering Bennet's resolve that he had done the right thing for Elizabeth by allowing her to be reared by his dear friend and his friend's wife. He was sure he owed them a debt of gratitude he could never repay.

I am here now, both willing and able to be a father to my daughter.

Amid a lull in the conversation, Mr. Bennet consulted his pocket watch.

Noticing this, Lady Anne said, "I am afraid I do not know what is keeping Elizabeth all this time."

"I am happy to go to her and find out," said Fitzwilliam.

Lady Anne Darcy loved her only son more than she loved life itself. She doted on him, in fact. He was meant for greatness; of that she was sure. Being the future master of Pemberley was really something, especially in that part of the world. True, her son was not a peer. Young Fitzwilliam

Darcy was, however, the grandson of a peer and the heir to one of the grandest estates in Derbyshire. If Lady Anne had her way, which she often did, he would also stand in line to inherit Rosings Park, one of the finest estates in Kent. Indeed, she and her sister, Lady Catherine de Bourgh, envisioned a glorious future for young Darcy. This future was sure to unfold with his marriage to Lady Catherine's daughter and Lady Anne's namesake, Miss Anne de Bourgh.

Lady Anne had not always known such happiness as now existed in her life. She had suffered more than her fair share of grief, in fact. She had desperately wanted a daughter. Several unsuccessful attempts and years later, her favorite wish unfolded with the birth of baby Georgiana. Lady Anne was robbed of her joy within days. An extended period of grief ensued. She dared not risk giving birth again. Not just because it was life-threatening for her to do so but because she simply could not bear the thought of suffering another such heartbreak as the loss of an infant would bring. There would never be another child —at least not her own.

Grief and sorrow, her constant companions, only began to fade away when she welcomed young Elizabeth into her home and heart. Despite the sorrow surrounding Elizabeth's circumstances, Lady Anne saw her as the blessing she had longed for. The one condition Thomas Bennet insisted upon was that he would never relinquish his parental rights. Not that the Darcys expected him to do so. It sufficed for the grieving couple to raise Elizabeth at Pemberley, providing her with the nurturing, care, and guidance that only a mother could offer—a task that Lady Anne was more than capable of undertaking.

Elizabeth and Lady Anne shared the same birthday, a remarkable occurrence that naturally forged a bond between them. They were kindred spirits—private, yet adventurous. Both possessed a love for books and held passionate beliefs. Their connection, akin to that of a mother and daughter, gradually grew as they supported each other through the trials of grief and the profound emotional wounds that followed. Lady Anne was convinced that Elizabeth considered Pemberley her home and the Darcys her family. However, she could not help but wonder and worry about Mr. Bennet's reappearance after so many years.

"You shall not, my son," Lady Anne declared firmly. "I shall have the honor." With that, her ladyship rose from her seat and made her way toward the door just as a servant opened it, allowing Elizabeth to enter.

Elizabeth offered a polite smile to Lady Anne. She expressed her apologies, saying, "I am sorry for keeping everyone waiting for dinner. I was so engrossed in my book that I lost track of time. Thank heavens for Mrs. Eastman," she added, referring to her paid companion.

"Come, dearest Elizabeth. Come and welcome our guest," Lady Anne said warmly, extending her hand.

Upon this invitation, Mr. Bennet stood up, capturing Elizabeth's attention for the first time. He cleared his throat, but before he could utter a word, Elizabeth's face drained of color.

"Papa..." she gasped, and then she fainted.

Chapter 2 - Intervention

As Elizabeth teetered on the brink of collapsing, Fitzwilliam sprang into action, reaching her just in time to prevent her fall. He cradled her fragile form in his arms, carefully lifting her and placing her gently on the settee. However, before he could tend to her further, his mother intervened, nudging him aside and taking charge of the situation.

A wave of powerlessness washed over the young man, an intense desire to care for Elizabeth himself. He watched as his mother fanned her and helped her regain consciousness. The sight of Elizabeth's shaken state pained him deeply.

Elizabeth cast a questioning glance at Fitzwilliam, who responded with a subtle nod, offering her reassurance in his presence. She redirected her eyes toward Lady Anne. Her voice was tinged with remorse. "I apologize. I do not know what came over me."

Adopting a soothing tone, Lady Anne replied, "There, there, my dear. You have experienced quite a shock, that is all."

Mr. Bennet, now hovering nearby, said, "It is I who should apologize. Undoubtedly, seeing your father after all these years is a complete surprise."

Elizabeth nodded. "Indeed, it is a surprise, sir ... though not unwelcome."

The wheels in Elizabeth's busy mind were moving at a rapid pace. Lady Anne always took extra care in keeping Elizabeth abreast of the comings and goings of Pemberley's guests. However, she had never mentioned that her father —the man who had abdicated his paternal responsibility toward her a decade prior—would be visiting. If Lady Anne knew he was coming, Elizabeth wondered why she had not told her.

Turning her eyes back to Lady Anne, Elizabeth asked, "Did you know of this in advance?"

Lady Anne nodded, her expression carrying a mix of understanding and compassion.

With curiosity brimming within her, Elizabeth

pressed further. "Why did you not inform me earlier, Lady Anne?"

Seeking to defend her ladyship, Mr. Bennet said, "You must not fault Lady Anne, my child. I insisted that my visit be kept a secret to protect you from disappointment if something unforeseeable were to prevent my being here."

Had the gentleman been looking in young Darcy's direction, he would have detected a slight roll of the young man's eyes. Elizabeth certainly noticed it. Not that she could find fault in Fitzwilliam's behavior. Who better than he understood the lasting impact of Elizabeth's upbringing, plagued by doubts about her father's love for her?

The elder Mr. Darcy rose from his seat, breaking the tension in the air. "Now that you are here, my friend, we shall have ample opportunity to get reacquainted, I am sure. But, for now, what say we adjourn to the dining room?"

After the conclusion of dinner, the gentlemen remained seated around the table, enveloped in the lingering aroma of tobacco, port, and the delicious scents of the meal. The room was filled with a comfortable, almost languid atmosphere. Once their threadbare conversation had run its course, Mr. Bennet and his longtime friend delved into a discussion about his plans for the visit.

"I always intended to bring my daughter to live with me at Longbourn. It is time for me to fulfill that promise."

Mr. Darcy nodded understandingly, his eyes reflecting a depth of empathy. "Of course," he said. "No one can fault you for wanting to do what you think is best for your daughter. My wife and I always knew it was a strong possibility that this day would come. Although I dare not speak for Lady Anne, for my part, as much as I will miss Elizabeth being here at Pemberley, I know she should spend time with you getting to know her true roots and the rest of her relatives. She has been a vital part of our family, and her absence will undoubtedly be felt."

"And you cannot know how much it means to me to have an ally in you. I suspect that not everyone here feels that way, my Lizzy included."

Mr. Bennet took a long puff of his cigar, the fragrant smoke curling around his features as he exhaled. He observed keenly that his plans did not garner the same approval from the son as they did from the father. Recalling the young man's conduct toward Elizabeth earlier in the drawing room and his attentive demeanor during dinner, Mr. Bennet could not help but ponder the true nature of their relationship. Moreover, he could not help but worry. True, he had left his daughter behind to be reared by the Darcys. Still, he knew his friend's ilk, especially Lady Anne Darcy's, and their expectations for their only son—Pemberley's heir. The last thing he wanted was for his daughter to suffer unreasonable expectations and disappointed hopes.

"I must confess her reaction upon seeing me is not exactly what I had hoped for."

"Are you referring to her fainting spell?" asked the elder Mr. Darcy.

"Yes, precisely. My arrival undoubtedly came as a shock to my daughter. I cannot say it was the initial response I had envisioned," Mr. Bennet replied, shifting his eyes in Fitzwilliam's direction. He added, "However, it was far better than the alternative, I suppose."

"The alternative, you say?"

Bennet nodded. "Indeed, my daughter could just as well have fled the room in disgust after coming face-to-face with the man who had left her when she was a child."

"I assure you, my friend, your daughter is

much too generous to condemn you for what happened in the past. We have done everything we could to assure Elizabeth of your love for her and to help her understand the situation. You believed you were doing what was best for her, being a single man with no family, to help raise her in a manner befitting a gentleman's daughter," said the elder Mr. Darcy.

Having observed his daughter throughout the evening, a mixture of pride and remorse washed over Mr. Bennet. "Seeing her tonight, a part of me has no regrets in that regard, for my Lizzy appears to be quite the accomplished young woman. However, I regret that I cannot boast of having any part in bringing that about. Indeed, that is my biggest regret in all of life."

"The material point is that you are here now," said his friend, emphasizing the importance of the present moment.

Bennet nodded. "Indeed, and I am resolved to do everything within my power to make amends for not being a part of my daughter's life for the past ten years."

Fitzwilliam cleared his throat. "I beg your pardon, Father," he began. "I am sure you agree it will be better to allow Elizabeth sufficient time to accustom herself to these unfolding developments before broaching the subject of her leaving Pemberley. This has been her home for the past decade. Leaving here ought to be her decision and hers alone."

Once the three gentlemen had concluded their indulgence in port and cigars, they made their way back to the elegant drawing room. Mr. Bennet, seizing an opportunity, persuaded Elizabeth to grace the company with a performance on the pianoforte. She found solace in this arrangement, for it allowed her to sit beside Fitzwilliam as he turned the pages, knowing that he would remain close by her side for the rest of the evening and thus preventing the opportunity for her to engage in awkward conversation with their guest, most of her memories of whom had long since faded away. She had always relied upon Fitzwilliam during uncomfortable times. Never had she felt more uncomfortable than she did at that moment with a father whom she did not know.

Elizabeth supposed that her relationship with her father would change during his visit. If she were to admit it, she was curious and intrigued to spend time with a man she had wondered about for years. Questions swirled within her—how could he have left her, how had he spent all those years, and would she ever truly know him? The thoughts of the mother and sister she had lost also lingered, but the absence of her father's presence plagued her the most. Why had he abandoned his paternal role, leaving her in the care of strangers? Did the sight of her remind him too much of the wife and child he had tragically lost? It pained her to entertain such thoughts, but they had become her constant companions, lingering like specters in her mind since childhood.

Elizabeth's mind was so busy with wonder and speculations that she could feel the beginning of a headache. She breathed a silent sigh of relief when the evening finally drew to a close and everyone adjourned to their respective quarters. Even if Fitzwilliam's apartment were not a short distance down the corridor from hers, she knew he would accompany her to her door. She was on the verge of turning her doorknob when Fitzwilliam covered her hand with his.

"I am here for you if you want to discuss all of this."

SIMPLY BEAUTIFUL

Elizabeth appreciated his support more than words could express. "I am grateful for that, Fitzwilliam, truly. But not tonight. I am rather weary. This evening has stirred up so many sentiments within me, and I need time to sort them out on my own."

"I understand. Pray, do not spend all night wrestling with your thoughts." He drew her into his arms for a comforting embrace. "Send for me if you need me. I will meet you in the library."

Elizabeth closed her eyes, leaning against Fitzwilliam's broad chest as he enveloped her in his arms. She felt the warmth of his body against hers, his arms providing a sense of security. The familiarity of his masculine scent brought her a measure of comfort, and the rhythmic beat of his heart against her ear soothed her troubled mind. At that moment, she felt safe and at peace—the calmest she had been throughout the entire evening.

"I will try not to disturb you," she said softly. "Tomorrow promises to be a long day. We both need our rest."

Fitzwilliam released her from his embrace but gently cupped her cheek, tilting her face to meet his gaze. "If I know you at all, you will surely rise before the break of dawn and embark on one of your solitary rambles." He paused, a tender smile tugging at his lips. "What if I were to accompany you?"

"I would like that very much indeed." Elizabeth's ensuing smile was the sincerest one that had crossed her face all evening. All her other smiles, it seemed, had been bestowed out of duty and obligation.

Fitzwilliam returned her smile, his eyes sparkling with anticipation. "Then it is settled. I shall meet you just before dawn. I will prepare our horses to ride to the Pointe if it meets with your approval. It has been too long since we watched the sunrise together."

Chapter 3 - Apprehension

Lady Anne lay in the opulent bed, her eyes fixed upon the rich red velvet canopy overhead. Its golden trim caught the flickering candlelight, casting a delicate glow throughout the room. Yet, despite the serene setting, her mind churned with apprehension.

Troubling thoughts and worries consumed her. She could not shake the unease that had settled in her stomach since Elizabeth's father had arrived at Pemberley. She had done her best to put on a brave face throughout the evening, but now that she and her husband were alone, she could not help but let her guard down.

"What are your thoughts on the evening, my

dear?" Lady Anne inquired, her voice filled with a mixture of curiosity and apprehension.

"I suppose it went as well as one could expect, given the circumstances," replied her husband.

"I suppose that is one way of looking at the events of the evening," she said, her gaze distant. "As good as could be expected, indeed."

Unsettling memories flooded her mind. Lady Anne recalled when she and her husband gave Elizabeth a miniature of her father's likeness. It was the first time that he had, in effect, let young Elizabeth down. Thomas Bennet had promised to visit Elizabeth on her tenth birthday, which would have been his first visit in two years. He had even written the child a letter announcing his intentions.

Except when the day of his arrival came, he was nowhere to be found. The only evidence of his existence was the arrival of his likeness with a hastily scribbled missive offering an excuse. Knowing how Bennet was living his life in Hertfordshire, Lady Anne half suspected he had not been the one to pen the letter.

Poor little Elizabeth's heart was broken. That would be the last time his neglect caused the child to suffer if Lady Anne had her way.

Letters from him were so few and far between that Lady Anne insisted by way of her husband that Mr. Bennet not even bother to write at all, for even something as innocuous as a missive was enough to alter Elizabeth's spirits for weeks, elevating her hopes that her father might come for a visit. Teaching the young child to hope and then to despair and agonize repeatedly was too much for anyone to bear, especially a child. Lady Anne would countenance it no more.

But now he had finally come, and she could not help but worry about what it meant.

The prospect that he meant to remove Elizabeth from Pemberley struck a disheartened chord in her. Lady Anne had made it the business of her life to see Elizabeth was well taken care of and had a bright future ahead of her, hence the supplementing of Elizabeth's dowry and her presentation at court.

Were Elizabeth to be removed from her care now, Lady Anne did not know what would become of Elizabeth's prospect for future felicity in marriage. From what she suspected of the limited society afforded in the rather small confines of Meryton in Hertfordshire, she could not imagine there would be anyone worthy of a young lady like Elizabeth.

Perhaps I am worrying too much, Lady Anne considered. *There is no reason why Elizabeth might not make an excellent match, perhaps to a gentleman beyond her sphere.* Maybe even a gentleman as honorable and decent as her son.

So long as it is not my son, she silently concluded before she blew out the candle by her bedside table and prepared for a good night's rest.

Except sleep did not come. There was too much to sort through as thoughts she had tucked into the back of her mind came to the fore, specifically the conversation she and her husband had shared about Elizabeth and Fitzwilliam some time ago.

"Mr. Darcy, I dare say it is not my imagination the manner in which our Elizabeth's spirits rise and fall with the timing of our son's arrival and departure from Pemberley of late."

"What are you suggesting, my dear?" asked Mr. Darcy without looking up from his morning paper.

"I am not suggesting anything but rather stating a fact. I fear Elizabeth's feelings for Fitzwilliam may lead to heartbreak on her part."

"Are you not persuaded that every single young lady in the land has an eye for Fitzwilliam?"

"I will not refute your assertion, but I am not referring to every young lady in this case. I am referring to Elizabeth. It is incumbent on us to protect her from needless pain, is it not?"

"What do you suggest we ought to do? Shall we ban Fitzwilliam from returning to Pemberley until he becomes officially engaged?"

"Of course I am not suggesting anything as extreme as that. But surely we ought to be thinking of both of their futures with more consideration. Fitzwilliam ought to have a tour of the continent soon, which will put some distance between them."

"With war raging on the continent, I do not see how it is possible."

"Well, there is that, but a young man of his age must travel and see various parts of the world before he is expected to settle down. My father and brother did, and I shall expect no less for my son. As for Elizabeth, I believe the time has come for her presentation at court. Once that is accomplished, she will be thrown in the path of many fine gentlemen, perhaps even a wealthy one at that, were we to augment her dowry."

"Presentation at court, you say. Are you certain that is something Elizabeth will go along with?"

"I do not see why she would not. It is what every young lady aspires to, is it not?"

"Every young lady in a position to enjoy such lofty aspirations, I suppose."

"And is Elizabeth any different from every such young lady? Besides, her presentation at court is a matter she and I have discussed many times. She knows how much I am looking forward to such a prospect."

"Well, you seem to have given this matter a great deal of thought, my dear."

"And why would I not? Is that not what someone of my stature does? Had our own daughter lived, I would surely have presented her at court at the proper time, and as Elizabeth is much like a daughter to me, I shall do no less than my duty toward her."

Further reflecting on the past, Lady Anne reminisced about Elizabeth's childhood, when taming her spirited nature resembled a formidable challenge. Even at a young age, Elizabeth possessed qualities that defined her as intelligent, inquisitive, and fiercely independent. Her inclination to indulge in long, solitary rambles exemplified her individuality. While Elizabeth prided herself on being an excellent walker, Mrs. Eastman, her paid companion, struggled to keep up. Lady Anne could not dissuade Elizabeth from embarking on pre-dawn excursions, but once daylight arrived, expectations changed. It was crucial to Lady Anne that Elizabeth conformed to the societal norms befitting her position as the ward of Pemberley's master and mistress.

Balancing Elizabeth's personality with society's expectations had been a constant struggle. Still, Lady Anne had persisted, ensuring Elizabeth received proper education and instruction from the best masters, allowing her to develop proficiency in drawing, painting screens, and showcasing her talent on the pianoforte. Her equestrian skills flourished under excellent guidance, despite Fitzwilliam introducing her to pony riding before she even turned ten. Such experiences fostered a close bond between the two youngest members of the Pemberley household, which remained unshakable despite the four-year age difference.

Lost in contemplation, Lady Anne gradually succumbed to slumber. The upcoming days held a weighty load of thoughts and preparations, requiring her to proceed with the utmost caution and strategic calculation. Elizabeth's destiny hung in the balance. Lady Anne vowed to exhaust every effort to secure it, pursuing a suitable union for

Elizabeth—one where she would be cherished and adored in a manner befitting her worth. Simultaneously, her ladyship remained resolute in safeguarding her son's future, tolerating no interference with her well-laid plans. Truly, a delicate affair indeed.

Chapter 4 - Confusion

THE NEXT MORNING, Elizabeth found herself awake before the break of dawn. She had tossed and turned all night, her mind unable to shake off the overwhelming emotions that had been stirred up by her father's sudden arrival. She had suffered a mix of joy, anger, and confusion, leaving her feeling drained and exhausted. A keen sense of urgency overcame her as she dressed in her riding outfit, for spending time alone with Fitzwilliam always enlivened her.

When she met him in the stable yard, he greeted her with a look of anticipation. "Good morning, Elizabeth. You look lovely this morning."

"Thank you, Fitzwilliam," she replied, trying to ignore the flutter in her stomach at the sight of him. It was not just his warm smile or impeccable riding outfit that made her heart skip a beat; it was how he always made her feel safe and protected whenever they rode out together. As they walked toward their horses, Elizabeth could not help but notice how his eyes lingered on her longer than usual.

As they prepared to ride out, Fitzwilliam approached Elizabeth's horse and held out a hand to help her mount. Once she was safe atop her horse, Fitzwilliam mounted his own, and they set off at a steady pace. Fitzwilliam kept a watchful eye on Elizabeth as they rode, even more protective than usual. Elizabeth could not help but feel comforted by his attentiveness.

The first rays of the rising sun painted the countryside in hues of gold as Elizabeth and Fitzwilliam rode toward the Pointe, their horses trotting at a leisurely pace. The gentle rhythm of their horses' hooves supplied a soothing backdrop to their conversation. Elizabeth opened up to her riding companion, telling him about her mixed emotions regarding her father's sudden arrival.

"It is just so peculiar, Fitzwilliam," she said, her voice betraying her confusion. "After all these years, he just shows up at Pemberley, expecting me to welcome him with open arms."

Fitzwilliam nodded sympathetically. "I can only imagine how difficult this must be for you, Elizabeth. Perhaps this is a chance for you to get to know him, to understand why he left."

She sighed. "Perhaps."

When they reached their destination, Elizabeth wandered to a nearby wooden bench, took a seat, and retrieved a miniature of her father's likeness while Fitzwilliam tended to the horses.

She was lost in thought, staring at her father's likeness, when Fitzwilliam sat beside her.

"I was wondering how you recognized your father so easily last evening," he said, leaning close to her.

She sighed. "I recall having studied my father's likeness for years upon first receiving it. It is a good thing indeed, for what a shame it would be not to recognize one's own relation—one's own father no less."

His eyes filled with empathy, Fitzwilliam nodded. "I am sure no one would find fault in you if you had. So many years have passed since you saw him last, and you were so young."

"Indeed. And now he is here at Pemberley. He

has returned—" Elizabeth's voice trembled slightly as she spoke. "But what does it mean, Fitzwilliam? Why has he chosen this moment to come back into my life? I cannot help but wonder..."

Elizabeth did not even know this man who had arrived at Pemberley. It had been a long time since she studied his miniature, having retrieved it from a box she had placed on a shelf in her closet more than six years ago. At first, she would retrieve the box from the chest and faithfully peruse its contents: letters, a book of poems, a bracelet that had belonged to her mother as well as her wedding ring, and her father's likeness.

She had a sense of what all those things signified—tokens meant to keep the memories of her past alive—these were meant to remind her of her past, her late mother, her late sister, and her father. In truth, her childhood memories had long since faded, replaced by her new life, her new family, for that was what the Darcys had become —her family in all the ways that mattered.

Though she had often considered the elder Mr. Darcy more of an uncle and Fitzwilliam—at least in the beginning—as more of an older, protective cousin, Elizabeth always thought of Lady Anne as a mother.

The years had taken their toll on her father's appearance judging by his likeness. She saw in his countenance a man who had suffered more than his fair share of grief and strife, and a part of her felt guilty over her not having been with him during the past years.

She confided as much to Fitzwilliam, and with a hint of guilt, concluding her declaration, she said, "I do not even know this man who has arrived at Pemberley. I have carried on with my life, building new bonds, while he remained a distant figure. I should not feel this way, should I? It was not for me to maintain a connection with him."

She tucked the miniature back inside her pocket and, staring off into the horizon, she folded one hand over the other in her lap. The weight of uncertainty hung in the air, and Elizabeth could not help but question what lay ahead. The conflicting emotions within her intensified as she grappled with the desire to understand her father and protect the life she had built at Pemberley—a delicate balance that would require careful navigation in the coming days.

. . .

Fitzwilliam reached out, his hand enveloping hers in a gentle squeeze before coaxing her to rest her head on his shoulder. The tranquil setting of the meadow surrounded them, its lush greenery dancing under the morning sunlight. Memories from a decade ago flooded Darcy's mind, recalling his first encounter with the young girl his parents had taken in.

He vividly remembered seeing her walk along the lane in the earliest hours, a habit he had adopted. Intrigued, he had wondered about her, this stranger who had awakened his protective instincts. On that fateful day, he had stumbled upon her, tears streaming down her face as she cradled her knees to her chest.

Elizabeth might not remember that one day he came across her crying. It was too long ago, and she was too young ... too distraught.

However, that day was seared into his memory —the urge to go to her, to comfort her, and to protect her.

How odd that she would rise before dawn and set off down the lane. What did a young girl know about such things? She ought to exercise better judgment, he had surmised. He decided to follow her from a safe distance—curious to know what she was about.

It was innocent enough, he had supposed. Someone had to protect her from harm. Heavens forbid that she might get lost wandering amid the woods. What if she were to fall?

Her crying had pained him severely. He moved closer still and heard her talking, but to whom was she speaking?

He could make out a few words amid her sobs: Mama, Sister, Jane, Papa, drawing him even closer. A twig cracked and summoned her attention, and she turned. She was not even startled to see him there; it was as if she knew he had been there all along.

Their eyes met, hers pooled with tears. "When is my papa coming back to get me?" she had asked, her voice trembling with vulnerability.

Blessed with a loving family, Fitzwilliam struggled to comprehend such deep sorrow. All he knew was that she was hurting, lost without a true home because home was where one's family lived.

Seeing none of the answers she searched for in his eyes, once again young Elizabeth burst into tears—still hugging her knees against her chest, slowly rocking herself back and forth to soothe herself.

Fitzwilliam's heart broke in two. He had seen his

own mother behave similarly, albeit years ago. It was on the heels of his baby sister's passing. He had witnessed his father comforting his mother, taking her in his arms and holding her close to his chest.

Fitzwilliam went to Elizabeth and sat down beside her. Taking her tiny hand in his, he held it and waited until her tears subsided.

"Have you seen my papa?" she had asked him after a while.

"I have not," he replied.

"Have you seen my mama and my sister?"

"Elizabeth," he said before falling silent. What was he to tell her? Did she not comprehend the reason her mother and sister, perhaps even her father, were never coming back?

"Fitzwilliam?" she asked, her voice imploring.

He wanted to ask her if she remembered anything from her past, but, for whatever reason, he did not feel it was his place. The last thing he had wanted to do was cause her further pain and distress by encouraging her to remember troubling aspects of her past. Perhaps one day, she would recall those events on her own, at which point he would be there to listen to her, providing his strength.

"My papa is not coming back, is he?" Elizabeth had asked, staring off into the far distance much the *same as she did presently.* "*Do you think he is dead too? Is that the reason he has not come to get me?*"

Young Fitzwilliam Darcy, feeling all the pain inherent in her words, had not known what to say.

He did the next best thing he knew to do. He placed his arm about young Elizabeth's shoulder, coaxed her into a caring embrace, and sat with her, and the two of them watched as the sun rose over the meadow. Whether her father was coming back to her or not, he could not say. He could say he would never allow her to suffer such pain, agony, sorrow, and helplessness ever again.

"*Do you not enjoy being here?*" *he recalled asking.*

"*I am scared, so scared. I do not like being all alone. I want my family. I want to go home now,*" *she had replied.*

"*Pray, do not be afraid, Elizabeth. You have nothing to fear. You have my father, my mother—you have me. We will not let anything happen to you. I will not let anything happen to you. You will never have to feel lonely again.*"

"*You will take care of me?*"

"*I will, Elizabeth. I promise. I will always take care of you.*"

. . .

That was ten years ago, and during all that time, Fitzwilliam never wavered, even though he only got a chance to spend time in company with her when he was home from school, which was few and far between.

His thoughts tended toward a more recent time—the day in London as he watched Elizabeth descend the stairs at Darcy House hours before being presented at court. He recalled thinking that protecting Elizabeth in Derbyshire was easy. Now that she was being presented at court, which he equated to being displayed on the marriage market, he knew his job of protecting her had really begun.

Elizabeth sighed, recalling him to the present. "I know you are correct, Fitzwilliam," she began, "about this being the chance for me to find out more about my father and perhaps even establish a connection with him. I just wish it did not feel so … so forced, I suppose. It is as though he can storm back into my life after all these years and expect me to forgive him for abandoning me."

Fitzwilliam reached over and took her hand, giving it a gentle squeeze. "I understand how you feel, Elizabeth. But do not forget that you have a choice in this. You can take all the time you need to come to terms with your feelings and decide what you want to do. No one can force you to do anything."

Elizabeth nodded, feeling grateful for his support and understanding. They sat in silence for a few long moments, taking pleasure in the beautiful surroundings. Elizabeth felt a sense of peace wash over her, the gravity of her emotions easing ever so slightly.

"I am grateful we came here, Fitzwilliam," she finally said, turning to face him with a glimmer of hope in her eyes. "This place is so serene and breathtaking. It is exactly what I needed this morning."

A gentle smile graced Fitzwilliam's lips as he looked closely at her. "Nature has a way of offering clarity and perspective. Sometimes, all we need is a moment of peace and quiet to sort through our thoughts and emotions."

As they made their way back to the manor house, Elizabeth felt a sense of renewed energy and purpose. She knew there would be trying times ahead, but she was determined to face them head-on. And with Fitzwilliam by her side, she felt like anything was possible.

As they parted ways at Pemberley Manor's

doorstep, Fitzwilliam took her hand and gave it a gentle squeeze. "Remember, Elizabeth, I am here for you. Whenever you need me, I am only a heartbeat away."

Elizabeth smiled at him, feeling a warmth spread through her chest. "Thank you, Fitzwilliam. I do not know what I would do without you."

Fitzwilliam leaned in and pressed a chaste kiss to her temple. "So long as it is within my power to protect you, you shall never have to find out."

Chapter 5 - Communication

THE FOLLOWING DAYS HURRIED BY. Elizabeth and Mr. Bennet were in a haze of activity. It was arduous to explain the reasons for his departure years prior while also trying to lay a foundation for their future as father and daughter. Nevertheless, Bennet found it amazing to share stories with her.

I sense a growing bond emerging between us, particularly over our shared love of reading. Indeed, it is an honor getting to know my Lizzy again.

Bennet could not have been more pleased by how his only child had turned out. Indeed, the Darcys had done an excellent job raising Elizabeth, just as they promised him they would when he made the gut-wrenching decision to leave her in their care at Pemberley a decade ago.

Elizabeth was indeed accomplished as one would have expected, having been raised by the daughter of an earl and one of the most esteemed gentlemen in Derbyshire.

If he could find but one fault in the arrangement, it was the close connection between Elizabeth and the Darcys' son and heir, Fitzwilliam. It did not sit well with him how close the two young people were, what with the young man being Elizabeth's senior by four years.

Bennet had long believed no such occasions existed for the two to grow so close, for a man at young Darcy's age was often away from his home. Surely someone of his stature, whose acquaintances were always increasing, had no reason to concern himself with his parents' ward during those opportunities that afforded his return to Pemberley.

The evidence before him suggested otherwise. Obviously, the young people were remarkably close. The young man was extremely attentive to Elizabeth, his eyes rarely straying from her. Likewise, Elizabeth seemed to rely too much on the young man, giving Bennet much cause for concern.

Bennet knew the Darcys too well for his

concern to be deemed unwarranted. He dared not speak for the young man and his feelings. He secretly wished the young man's doting on Elizabeth was akin to an older, overly protective brother.

Young Darcy, no doubt, deems me a threat to my own daughter. Keeping a watchful eye on her when we are together, even from a distance, as though he were jealous because his presumed role as Elizabeth's longtime protector diminishes with each passing day.

As for Elizabeth's feelings, Bennet was not so sure. Young girls want nothing more than to be in love, and the look he saw in his daughter's eyes whenever she looked at young Darcy evinced all the telltale signs of infatuation. What a precarious position in which to find oneself.

Bennet knew enough about Lady Anne Darcy and her ilk to know that she would never countenance an alliance between her only son and Elizabeth. It did not matter that she raised Elizabeth and the connection between them could be likened to that of a mother and daughter. He knew that Lady Anne had far grander plans for her son's future. She had decided long ago who the next mistress of Pemberley would be. Only a young woman with a large fortune and noble blood coursing through her veins would be deemed good enough for young Darcy. Said person was firmly settled in Lady Anne's mind as her niece and namesake, Miss Anne de Bourgh.

Who that knew the noble lady did not know that? No doubt young Darcy would honor his mother's favorite wish for him. That was simply how it was for people of their ilk who often entertained the idea of marriage for wealth and connection instead of marriage based on love.

Why, even the Darcys' marriage had been born out of an arrangement, with Gerald Darcy's large fortune more than compensating for his lack of nobility.

His daughter Elizabeth had not a single drop of noble blood as far as Thomas Bennet knew. She surely had no fortune. *No, Lady Anne will never accept Lizzy as a potential daughter-in-law.*

So, where does that leave my daughter if it is indeed true that she is in love with the young heir? Bennet silently questioned. Ripe for future heartbreak was the only conclusion he could draw, leading him to but one decision.

I must carry my Lizzy away from all this before it is too late and she ends up suffering from a broken heart brought on by disappointed hopes.

Bennet could have no doubt that he had been Elizabeth's greatest source of disappointment for the past several years. All of the promises he had made were promises subsequently broken.

Truth be told, every time he resolved to put the past behind him and bury the memories of the fatal carriage accident that had altered his world in such a devastating and tragic way, his troubles would assail him, returning with a vengeance. They denied him and robbed him of his resolve to be a better man and a better father, without fail, every single time.

All of that is behind me now, now that I know what I must do. My Lizzy does not belong here living among these people. She belongs at Longbourn Village, where she was born and reared for the first part of her life, amid her own kin.

It had been over a year since he had had his last drink. He had even forgone imbibing port with his friend after dinner, opting for conversation instead—confirmation of his having conquered his demons once and for all. Now he was even more determined to be the type of father who would protect his daughter. The kind of father she deserved.

He stared out the window and took in the

sweeping landscape. Pemberley was indeed a magnificent estate.

I cannot give her all this, but I can provide her with something far better, in my humble opinion. I can give her a sense of her own self, her roots, a place where she really belongs.

Mr. Bennet settled into the leather armchair in Pemberley's library, his crinkled hands clasped over the rich leather binding of a book. He sighed as he looked up at his daughter, who had been browsing the shelves restlessly.

"Lizzy," he said tentatively, "it is time for you to return to Longbourn."

Elizabeth took a deep breath and turned to face her father. The thought of leaving Pemberley and the company of Fitzwilliam was unbearable. While with him, Elizabeth reveled in each passing moment, savoring the simple pleasures they shared. Whether it was their leisurely strolls along winding lanes, engrossed in captivating discussions, or the peaceful hours spent immersed in the sanctuary of the library, their togetherness brought her immeasurable joy. Her heart raced as she thought of the last few days, especially in the wake of her father's unexpected arrival—the intimate intercourse, the ever tightening bond between them, and the subtle gestures that whispered volumes of unspoken affection.

Elizabeth raised an eyebrow. "Longbourn? But I have been perfectly content here at Pemberley. I am not certain I should wish to leave."

Her father sighed. "Yes, you have lived here for the past ten years, but Pemberley is not your true home. Longbourn is where you belong, where our family has lived for generations. It is time for your return to Hertfordshire."

He began speaking of Longbourn and the long-forgotten childhood memories it held for Elizabeth. Bennet knew deep in his heart that she belonged at Longbourn, and he held fast to the possibility that she might remain there long after his time had expired. What solace this brought to his mind—to know his only child would always have a place in the home that he and his family had resided in their entire lives.

"I can hardly object to your wanting to leave me such a legacy, but did you not say the estate is entailed to the male line of the family? Surely you do not mean for the gentleman to choose me as his wife. Who is to say he is not married?"

"I can assure you the gentleman is not only single but is also in want of a wife. As it happens, he wrote to me not very long ago with the express intent of wishing for an introduction to you, my Lizzy. The entail has been quite a bone of contention, especially with my not having a son. I do, however, have you, and through no fault of your own, my demise would leave you in a most disadvantageous position. I believe this is the young man's way of wanting to make amends for the circumstances of the entail."

Elizabeth's mouth gaped. "Papa! Have you agreed to an arranged marriage between me and Longbourn's heir apparent?"

He shook his head. "That is not what I am saying, but if I were, surely the concept of arranged marriages is not foreign to you, what with the future marriage between Pemberley's heir and his cousin being so widely known and expected. But no, my Lizzy, I am not saying that you have to marry this accommodating fellow, but it would mean the world to me if you would consent to meet with him."

"Pray, is this the reason for your being here at

Pemberley after all this time? Do you mean to bring me to Hertfordshire simply to throw me in the path of Longbourn's heir, hoping that I can be persuaded to accept his hand in marriage in order to fulfill your parental ambition of seeing me settled at Longbourn?"

"It is time for you to accept the realities of our situation. The Darcys are fine, upstanding people, else I would not have left you with them, but they are not like us."

"How are we so different? You are a gentleman. I am a gentleman's daughter. That must certainly make all of us equals."

"Lady Anne Darcy is indeed a gentleman's wife, but she is also the daughter of a peer. She is of noble blood, and despite how much she clearly cares for you, she does not view you as a suitable wife for her only son, the grandson of an earl. And I fear the longer you remain here the harder it will be for you to accept when she makes her preferences clear."

"I ... I am not sure I know what you mean."

The leather chair's bindings creaked as Bennet shifted his weight slightly and leaned forward, his countenance laced with concern. "I think you do, Lizzy. You might not want to admit it, but I have seen how you look at young Darcy. And I have seen the way he looks at you. You are a bright, beautiful young woman, and I do not mean to stand idly by and watch you suffer disappointed hopes."

"I believe you may have read more into my expectations than is warranted," Elizabeth said, although her thoughts were along a different vein altogether. *Have my feelings for Fitzwilliam been so obvious or so much on display as my father believes? So poorly disguised?*

Eyeing Elizabeth quizzically, Mr. Bennet concluded, "Then there is even more reason for you to embrace the idea of returning to Hertfordshire, your true home, where your relations who are longing to know you better wait for you."

Elizabeth remained silent for a moment, her mind whirling with shifting thoughts and emotions. On the one hand, she could not bear the thought of leaving Pemberley, and Fitzwilliam, behind. On the other hand, she could not deny the importance of her family and heritage, of which Longbourn was a significant part. To further complicate matters was the underlying tension between her and her father, a man whom she hardly even knew, and the niggling notion that he was trying to control her life and make decisions for her. Decisions that were not his to make as far as she was concerned.

Despite the turmoil in her mind, Elizabeth settled on the notion deep down inside that her father was only looking out for her best interests as he had done in allowing her to be reared by the Darcys in the first place. He had never meant for the arrangement to be permanent, and this was his way of proving it.

"I understand what you are saying, Papa," she finally said, her voice soft. "However, the prospect of leaving Pemberley, the only home that holds actual memories for me, is daunting to say the least and not a decision that I am able to make in haste. I must beg for your indulgence."

Mr. Bennet looked relieved but also a little sad. "You must take all the time you need. I know a decision to leave the place you have long called home will not be easy, but I believe it is the right thing to do."

Elizabeth had always thought she wanted her father to return to Pemberley. Why had he come now after so many years? Why now?

After so many years of his absence, she would

have contented herself with the occasional visit. After so many years of neglect, he sat there with the look in his eyes she had long since forgotten, telling her he wanted to bring her to his home in Hertfordshire to live with him. Was it wrong of her to distrust his intentions? He wanted to take her away from Derbyshire, which was her home—to take her away from Fitzwilliam. Fitzwilliam, whom she never wished to be parted from, whom she had taught herself to believe would always be central to her life.

The turmoil in her mind increased with every review of her circumstance.

She had no words, her eyes flickering over the shelves of books in the library, the ones Fitzwilliam had recommended to her and the ones they had read together. She wondered what would become of the bond between them if she left Pemberley, and her heart ached at the thought.

Chapter 6 - Champion

Elizabeth's father's unexpected return had brought with it a flood of conflicting emotions. There were moments when she reveled in the warmth of their rekindled relationship, sharing her dreams and fears with the man who had once been absent from her life. Yet, beneath the surface, a flicker of anger and betrayal by his abandonment remained, casting shadows upon her newfound bond with him.

Through all of this emotional turmoil, Fitzwilliam Darcy stood tall and resolute, a pillar of strength amid the storm; his presence brought a sense of calm and reassurance, as if the air around him radiated unwavering support. He listened as she poured out her heart, offering his own insights and perspectives on the situation. And whenever she needed an escape, he was always there to accompany her on long walks or rides, helping her clear her mind and find balance once again.

But as the days turned into weeks, Elizabeth grew increasingly restless. She could not shake off the feeling that something else was missing, that there was more to life than just playing the role of a dutiful daughter.

During one of their leisurely rides across the sprawling estate, Fitzwilliam's keen eyes caught the glimmer of unrest in Elizabeth's eyes. Their horses slowed to a gentle trot, their hooves sinking into the rich earth, as he turned his attention to her, a mixture of concern and understanding etched upon his countenance.

"What is it, Elizabeth?"

Elizabeth glanced at her companion, her eyes searching his face for understanding. "Fitzwilliam, I feel torn between my duty and my desires. My father's sudden return has stirred up a whirlwind of emotions within me. Part of me wants to embrace the life he envisions for me at Longbourn, but another part of me yearns for something more, something beyond the boundaries of societal expectations."

Fitzwilliam's brow furrowed with concern. "I sense your restlessness, Elizabeth. And I understand your desire for more than what society dictates. You are a remarkable woman with a thirst for knowledge and adventure. Your love for books and how your eyes light up when we discuss new ideas speaks volumes about the depth of your spirit."

Elizabeth smiled gratefully, touched by his compassion. "Thank you, Fitzwilliam. You have always seen me for who I am, beyond the superficial expectations placed upon me. I feel a connection with you that I cannot deny, and it adds to my dilemma. My heart longs for the freedom to explore faraway places, to engage in intellectual pursuits, and to be with someone who understands and supports my aspirations."

Fitzwilliam's eyes softened. "Elizabeth, I want nothing more than for you to be happy, to realize your dreams, and find fulfillment in life. If Longbourn is not where your heart truly lies, I will remain by your side no matter where your journey takes you. Whatever you decide, I would never stand in the way of your happiness."

Her heart fluttered at his words, and she took a moment to gather her thoughts. "Fitzwilliam, you have always been a source of strength and inspiration to me. Your unwavering support and understanding mean the world to me. But I cannot ignore the ties with my father that have begun to mend. Leaving Pemberley feels like leaving a part of myself behind, especially knowing the possible consequences of disappointing Lady Anne." Her voice low, she said, "That is to say nothing of the thought of leaving you, which fills me with a bittersweet ache, but I know deep down that I must follow the path that calls to me, wherever it may lead."

Reaching out, Fitzwilliam gently took hold of her hand. "Elizabeth, I cannot predict the twists and turns that lie before us, but I know this with every fiber of my being: love should never be compromised. If your heart leads you to Longbourn, you have my support, embracing whatever decision you make. Our bond is unbreakable, even in the face of separation. Time and distance cannot diminish that."

He brought her hand to his lips, pressing a tender kiss against her knuckles. "So, Elizabeth, let us cherish the time we have now and trust that our bond will endure. Trust in the unpredictability of life, for it has a way of intertwining our destinies when we least expect it. Wherever you go, whatever choices you make, I will forever be here, unwavering in my devotion."

A mixture of gratitude and melancholy danced within Elizabeth's heart. She understood the road ahead would be filled with uncertainty, demanding difficult choices and sacrifices. Yet, she clung to the knowledge that Fitzwilliam stood as her staunchest ally, a steadfast supporter who cherished her unconditionally.

As they resumed their ride, the wind whispered secrets of change and possibility, and Elizabeth could not help but feel a sense of hope. She silently vowed to embrace her future with courage and follow the untrodden path that beckoned, even if it meant leaving Pemberley and Fitzwilliam behind, if only for a while.

Chapter 7 - Machinations

Lady Catherine de Bourgh's arrival at Pemberley took Lady Anne by surprise. The formidable lady entered the grand estate with an air of authority, commanding attention with every step she took. Her towering presence filled the room, her imposing figure draped in rich fabrics that rustled with each movement. Her coiffed curls, meticulously arranged, bounced against her powdered face, framing features that bore the marks of a lifetime of privilege and assertiveness.

Lady Catherine's countenance displayed a regal smirk, as if she had been graced with a permanent expression of superiority. Her piercing eyes, sharp and calculating, surveyed the surroundings with an unabashed curiosity that demanded acknowledgment. Her lips, adorned with a hint of disdain, seemed eternally poised to deliver a biting remark.

Exuding confidence and self-assuredness, Lady Catherine gracefully settled into the plush armchair of the opulent drawing room. A servant approached with a delicate china cup, offering her a steaming cup of fragrant tea. With a regal nod, Lady Catherine accepted the beverage, the porcelain clinking softly against her bejeweled fingers.

Despite being sisters, the two women could not have been more different. Lady Catherine was fiercely independent, domineering, and had always been the favorite of their father. On the other hand, Lady Anne was gentle, reserved and had always been overshadowed by her sister's strong disposition.

Growing up, Lady Anne had always admired her older sister's poise and confidence. Still, as they grew older, Lady Catherine's domineering personality began to grate on her. Lady Catherine always seemed to think she knew what was best for everyone, including Lady Anne.

However, they always agreed that their children were designed for each other at birth and destined to be married. Indeed, it was both of the sisters' favorite wishes.

"Had I known you were coming, I would have arranged a proper welcome," said Lady Anne, her voice laced with a mix of surprise and hospitality.

Lady Catherine's eyes widened. "Surely you could not expect me to leave Derbyshire without calling on you, dearest Anne." Her words held a hint of superiority as if she believed herself entitled to be present in every aspect of her sister's life.

Lady Anne sighed inwardly. "No, I do not suppose you would."

Their conversation turned to family matters, and Lady Anne inquired about their relatives in Matlock.

"Our brother and the countess are as well as can be expected," she replied with an air of detachment.

"And what of my niece, Anne? Does she remain in Matlock?"

"No, Anne arrived with me," Lady Catherine responded, a hint of genuine affection seeping through her stern demeanor. "However, owing to her health and the challenge of traveling, she was obliged to go directly to her usual apartment with her companion, Mrs. Jenkinson."

Lady Anne nodded, her thoughts drifting to the young woman's delicate constitution and its inherent constraints. "I shall look forward to seeing my dear niece at dinner. You are aware that we have a houseguest, are you not?"

"I assure you that nothing of consequence escapes my notice," Lady Catherine replied. "Elizabeth must be pleased to be reunited with her father—such that he is—after all these years."

Lady Catherine had always held a peculiar fondness for the little girl whom Lady Anne had taken into her home and treated as her own daughter. Perhaps, had the young girl and Lady Catherine's daughter Anne got along better, Lady Catherine would have liked her even more. Maybe she would have perceived Elizabeth as less of a threat—a ticking bomb set to explode in just a matter of time.

It was nothing to do with Elizabeth personally. She regarded any young girl as a threat to her daughter. Anne was a sickly child. She was born that way. Thus, she could never run, jump, and play like the other children. This disparity was most evident when Lady Catherine would bring Anne to Pemberley during the summers or Matlock and likewise when the Darcys visited Kent.

Young Elizabeth suffered no such affliction with her wild animal spirits, which was evidenced by her lack of patience to remain indoors with Anne. Elizabeth had much rather be outside with the boys doing the things boys were most often known to do. Things like riding horses and even fishing.

Elizabeth's temperament proved quite disadvantageous for Anne, for whereas Fitzwilliam doted on Elizabeth, he scarcely paid any attention at all to his cousin. Lady Catherine was more than a little bothered to see that. If it were not for the fact that Anne and her nephew were promised to each other from their cradles, Lady Catherine might have been seriously displeased.

Lady Catherine, who was widely celebrated for her frankness in character, made sure to remind her sister of the promise they made when the children were born whenever she could.

"Mind you, Sister, to have a care where my nephew and your ward are concerned, especially now that they are older. You know my feelings on the subject. Those two have always been much too cozy with each other for my taste. Neither of them pays any attention at all to my Anne when they are all in company, for they are too busy paying attention to each other."

"In all honesty, Anne is so different from Fitzwilliam and even Elizabeth, for that matter, despite her and the latter being of the same sex."

"Anne's health will not allow her to be as outgoing and energetic as others close to her in age, but that can hardly be an excuse for them to ignore her in preference for each other all the time."

Lady Anne well imagined Elizabeth supposed she was doing a fairly decent job of hiding her tender feelings for Fitzwilliam when, in fact, she was fooling no one at all. But a young girl of her age in the presence of a tall, handsome young man with all the best parts of beauty and everything in his favor; if that was not a recipe for infatuation, then what was? Confiding her true sentiments, even to a most beloved sister, was not part of Lady Anne's plan.

"I posit their closeness is merely a symptom of their shared upbringing," she said, wrestling with her conflicting feelings. "When they are together, they are accustomed to disregarding the feelings of others."

"That is a problem in and of itself, is it not? It is up to us to teach them to treat others with more consideration, or else we will be terribly remiss. But I know you, Sister. You are wont to give Fitzwilliam far too much liberty. I, on the other hand, suffer no such failing. I shall gladly take him aside and enlighten him about his misguided ways."

"Pray do no such thing, Sister. I am sure Mr. Darcy would consider it impertinent were you to take it upon yourself to influence our son or interfere with his role as a parent. That is to say nothing of how it would make me feel."

Lady Catherine scoffed. "I do not see why either of you should take offense. Are we not family? And since when are our children off limits when it comes to giving them good principles to follow? I would take no such offense were either of you to counsel my Anne. Not that she would ever require such guidance, for she embodies loyalty, kindness, and all that is good in the world. She is completely without fault."

"Then that is your good fortune, I suppose. As

for my son, I would never say he is completely without fault. Still, I will stipulate that he will not be affected by the will of others, even by those closely connected to him."

"I fear you will regret ever espousing such nonsense, Sister. But I shall speak no more on the subject. So long as Fitzwilliam is mindful of his duty to marry my Anne, I shall have no cause to repine."

"Fear not, Catherine, for I assure you, in that regard, Fitzwilliam knows exactly what he must do. He will not disappoint either of us. You have my word."

"Had you simply put the young woman in her own establishment in town after her coming out season, we would not be having this discussion," Lady Catherine opined. "But none of that matters now as I have taken matters into my own hands."

"What have you done?" Lady Anne asked, her eyes fixed on her sister, searching for answers she was not sure she wanted to find.

Lady Catherine peered over her cup of fragrant tea with a haughty smirk as she glanced around the drawing room at Pemberley. Her sister stared back at her with a quizzical eye.

"I feel I ought to congratulate myself for my scheme to separate Elizabeth from Fitzwilliam is unfolding exactly as I had planned," she drawled. "The beauty of it all is that my new vicar, Mr. William Collins, and your sudden houseguest have no reason to suspect my involvement."

Lady Anne set down her cup with a clatter. "What on earth are you saying? Elizabeth is like a daughter to me. Please tell me you have not done anything to harm her!"

A triumphant gleam flickered in Lady Catherine's eyes as she leaned back in her chair, basking in her perceived victory. "Must I remind you that all your efforts to throw Elizabeth in the path of worthy gentlemen have been in vain? No young woman of her sphere can boast of such a grand coming out as she enjoyed. More than one suitor tried to turn her head, and none of them could tempt her. And how could they, for I doubt a duke could capture her fancy so long as she has her sights set on our Fitzwilliam."

Even if Lady Anne agreed with her sister's sentiments, she dared not confess it aloud, for she would do nothing to fuel Lady Catherine's ire toward Elizabeth.

"You concern yourself too much about the feelings between Elizabeth and my son. Fitzwilliam knows better than to increase a young woman's expectations when he is clearly meant for his cousin Anne."

"For heaven's sake, Sister. You must open your eyes and see what is happening between those two. That is precisely why I have taken measures to put considerable distance between them."

"I am not sure I wish to know what you have done."

"That may be, but I shall tell you all the same. I have long kept myself attuned to the goings on with Thomas Bennet ever since he left his young daughter behind to be reared alongside my nephew. Even then, I suspected he had ulterior motives. What person in his position would not wish to see a daughter well-settled?"

Lady Anne could not help but give some credence to her sister's speculation. A secret that she had shared with no one—not even her husband—haunted her to that day. It tore at her heart when she glimpsed the unmistakable grief on Elizabeth's face.

The remembrance of a heated exchange with Mrs. Bennet, Elizabeth's late mother, echoed in

Lady Anne's thoughts. The impact of what had been said pained her to that day, even though she had meant every single word of it. The Bennet family were visiting Pemberley, and after having listened to Mrs. Bennet go on and on about what a good thing it would be if one of her daughters were to marry the heir to Pemberley for what seemed the hundredth time during her visit, her ladyship could take no more.

Having reached the end of her patience listening to such a foolish supposition, Lady Anne told the silly woman that under no circumstances would she ever countenance the marriage of her son, Pemberley's heir, to the daughter of someone whose roots were in trade.

"*Are the shades of Pemberley to be thus polluted?*" Lady Anne had exclaimed.

"*My daughters, despite whatever my own family roots may be, are the daughters of a gentleman, which must surely make them equal to any gentleman whom they shall meet,*" Mrs. Bennet cried.

"*There are gentlemen, and there are gentlemen. My son, being of noble blood, is not one such man. Not only is he the future heir to all this, but he is the grandson of a peer. I am afraid, my dear, your daughters are not and will never be equal to my son.*"

"But my own husband—"

Lady Anne had held up her hand. "No! I will not tolerate any further discussion on this matter. Suffice it to say I have my own plans for my son—plans that will not be disrupted by someone of inferior birth."

"Why, I have never been so disrespected in all my life," said Mrs. Bennet in response to Lady Anne's outright dismissal of a future alliance between one of her daughters and Pemberley's heir.

Seeing that the woman was offended, Lady Anne said, "Pray do not take my words the wrong way. I only mean to apprise you of the realities of our world so that you do not raise your daughters to aspire to stations in life beyond that which they were born to. As charming as your girls will likely turn out to be, they are unlikely to attract men of any real consequence in the world owing to their low standing."

She recalled pausing and taking a sip of hot tea before she had concluded, "Despite their being a gentleman's daughters."

For all intents and purposes, that was the last conversation the two ladies had with each other. Mrs. Bennet had been so offended by someone she believed to be a kindred spirit that she had insisted that her family quit Pemberley within the hour. Why on earth would she wish to stay in a place where she and her daughters were deemed inferior?

Neither of the ladies was of a mind to consider the feelings of the other, and the ladies' parting was marked not by the cordiality of friends but by a silent disdain of enemies.

The next time Lady Anne would have cause to give serious thought to Mrs. Bennet was when she found herself tasked with rearing the late mother's surviving child.

Raising a daughter had been her favorite wish for so long, and now she had the chance to realize it. She could not possibly refuse, but neither could she rid herself of the guilt she carried, having injured the hopes of the woman whose tragic death had been the means of bringing it about.

To that day, Lady Anne had not wavered in her stance. Fate had seen fit to allow a Bennet daughter to be reared at Pemberley as her own. Still, a Bennet daughter would never be mistress of Pemberley, despite how much she had grown to love Elizabeth.

"As you are aware, Catherine," Lady Anne began, "Elizabeth has a dowry of twenty thousand pounds. She will indeed make an excellent match, even if it takes longer than you wish."

"You know my character. I am not one to leave such things to chance. Not when the future of my own daughter's happiness is at stake. That said, you must allow me to tell you what I have done. In fact, once you hear it, you shall have no cause at all to worry about Elizabeth's future."

Lady Catherine espoused the lengths she had pursued to locate the heir to Thomas Bennet's estate and offer him the living in Hunsford. She then persuaded him to find a wife, giving him the strongest hint that he ought to choose Mr. Bennet's daughter as a means of amending the circumstances of the entail of the gentleman's estate away from the female line. As malleable as Mr. Collins proved to be, Lady Catherine persuaded him with little effort, and the gentleman wrote to Mr. Bennet declaring his intentions and the rest, Lady Catherine said, needed no more explanation.

"And now you may thank me," said Lady Catherine. "My efforts led to Mr. Bennet's being here, and soon Elizabeth's marital prospects will be that gentleman's concerns. All will be right with the world."

Concerned, Lady Anne rubbed her hand against her forehead.

Lady Catherine rolled her eyes. "Do not be so sentimental, Anne. I fear you may allow your sentiments to cloud your judgment. Elizabeth may have been raised with our family, but she is not one of us. She is a Bennet and belongs with those of her own sphere."

Lady Anne fell silent, her thoughts turning to Elizabeth. She had grown to love the girl as if she were her own daughter, and the idea of sending her away was almost unbearable. But Lady Catherine was correct—Elizabeth was not truly a member of their family. Her father had every right to exercise measures to secure his daughter's future just as she was bound and determined to ensure her son's.

"Very well," she said quietly. "But please, Catherine, do not let any harm come to Elizabeth. She deserves better than that."

Lady Catherine waved a dismissive hand. "Of course, of course. You worry too much, Anne. Elizabeth will be fine. And who knows? Perhaps this separation will do her good. She needs to understand that there is more to life than just Pemberley and Fitzwilliam."

Lady Anne's heart sank at her sister's words. She knew Lady Catherine was not one to be trifled with, but she could not help but feel a sense of foreboding over what was in store for Elizabeth. Who was this Mr. Collins? True, he was a vicar, but did that make him a good man worthy of Elizabeth? Lady Anne could only hope and pray.

Chapter 8 - Conversation

Dinner at Pemberley that evening was a lavish affair, befitting the estate's grandeur. The expansive dining room exuded elegance, its walls adorned with exquisite paintings and tapestries that depicted scenes of stateliness and sophistication. The large table, draped in fine linen, was meticulously set with sparkling china, gleaming silverware, and delicate crystal glasses, each item reflecting the soft glow of the candlelight that danced in the room.

On one side of Elizabeth sat her father and on the other Mrs. Eastman. Lady Catherine sat opposite her daughter Anne, relying on Anne's companion Mrs. Jenkinson to address her faint whispers. The elder Mr. Darcy and Lady Anne sat at opposite ends of the exquisite mahogany table. Fitzwilliam was nowhere to be found.

Where is Fitzwilliam? Lady Anne wondered more than once. She tried to remain composed as best she could but could not help but steal glances at the empty chair beside Lady Catherine as if expecting him to arrive at any moment. *My son may run from his familial duty to marry his cousin, but he cannot hide.*

As the evening progressed, the atmosphere in the room settled into a comfortable rhythm. The clinking of silverware and the murmur of conversations blended harmoniously. The tantalizing aroma of sumptuous dishes wafted through the air, tempting the guests' palates. Yet, despite the outward appearance of cordiality, Lady Anne could not shake the gnawing unease that had settled within her since her earlier conversation with Lady Catherine.

Her eyes lingered on Elizabeth, who was engaged in animated conversation with her father. The young woman's expressive eyes sparkled with intelligence and a quick wit that Lady Anne admired. A pang of regret tugged at her heart as she imagined the prospect of Elizabeth leaving Pemberley. She had grown to cherish Elizabeth as her own daughter, and the thought of her being whisked away to marry a man of whom Lady Anne knew so little filled her with a sense of unease and apprehension.

Amid the festivities, it was no surprise that Lady Catherine soon took center stage, commanding the conversation with tales of her accomplishments and the alleged triumphs of her daughter, Anne, if only her health would allow it.

Thomas Bennet sat silently, his observant eyes scanning the room, taking in every minute detail. He was a man of few words, but his sharp wit and intelligence were evident in his piercing eyes that flickered with amusement. As Lady Catherine droned on, her voice suffused with a sense of self-importance, he leaned toward Elizabeth and whispered, "It appears her ladyship fancies herself an expert on all things."

Elizabeth stifled a laugh, her hand delicately covering her mouth. "Indeed, she does," she replied, her voice hushed.

This moment of amusement with his daughter brought a sense of joy to Mr. Bennet. The connection they shared in finding humor in the absurdity of others' behavior was a source of delight.

Elizabeth said, "But, I must admit, her tales of Anne's accomplishments do make me feel rather inadequate in comparison."

Bennet chuckled softly, appreciating his daughter's sentiment. "I understand she would have been a great proficient on the pianoforte."

A mischievous grin played on Elizabeth's lips. "Yes, I have heard so as well. It is a shame that her health does not permit her to display her talents."

Bennet nodded.

No doubt displeased that not every ear in the room was listening to what she had to say, Lady Catherine said, "What is that the two of you are discussing among yourselves, Elizabeth?"

Elizabeth quickly straightened up in her seat, turning to face Lady Catherine with a forced smile. "Oh, just the beauty of Pemberley, your ladyship," she lied smoothly. "We were admiring the art on the walls."

Lady Catherine huffed, clearly not believing a word of it. "Well, I suppose that is a suitable topic of conversation for young ladies. However, I must remind you that there are more important things to discuss than mere aesthetics. For example, the importance of marrying well and securing a good future for oneself."

Elizabeth's smile faltered and her eyes flickered over to her father. He had gone rigid, his eyes narrowed, and his jaw clenched tight.

"Of course, your ladyship," Elizabeth said, her voice strained. "I shall keep that in mind going forward."

Lady Catherine nodded, satisfied with the response, and continued on with her conversation, this time directed toward Anne. But Elizabeth could not shake the anger and frustration that had settled in her chest. She despised the way Lady Catherine always spoke of marriage as if it were a business transaction, with no regard for love or happiness.

As the conversation continued, Elizabeth struggled to suppress the irritation teeming inside her. She listened, growing increasingly impatient with every passing moment, as Lady Catherine espoused the virtues of pedigree and wealth in securing a suitable match. If she had to endure one more account of how her daughter and her nephew were destined for each other and how their marriage would fulfill the wishes of both mothers, Elizabeth feared she might scream.

Is there any wonder Fitzwilliam is away from Pemberley this evening, having traveled to Matlock?

Elizabeth suspected he had purposely left the estate upon the arrival of his aunt and cousin, seeking respite from pressing inquiries about when he intended to fulfill his familial obligation to marry his cousin. However, having spent the day in his company, riding horseback and picnicking in the idyllic meadow, Elizabeth could have no cause to complain.

As for Miss Anne de Bourgh, Elizabeth was in the habit of seeing the young heiress at least three or four times a year. She, too, was Elizabeth's senior by several years. Miss Anne de Bourgh, whom Elizabeth always called Miss Anne since the day they first met, and there never existed a reason to drop the deferential appellation in the ensuing years, was a pale and sickly sort of creature who enjoyed less than her fair share of beauty—quite in contrast to her beautiful aunt Lady Anne and her rather handsome mother Lady Catherine.

Despite their familial connection, Fitzwilliam showed no evidence of affection for his cousin Anne. Truth be told, Elizabeth could detect scant evidence on Anne's part of fondness toward Fitzwilliam, causing her to suspect that Lady Anne's favorite wish for her son was nothing more than a candle in the wind. Even the faintest gust would disappoint the hopes of quite a few people, as even the Fitzwilliam family nurtured the hope according to Elizabeth's best observations.

But then, just as Lady Catherine was launching into yet another tirade about the benefits of marrying within one's own social circle, Mr. Bennet cleared his throat loudly, interrupting her mid-sentence.

"Lady Catherine, might I suggest that we change the subject?" he asked, his tone polite but firm. "I fear all this talk of marriage is growing tiresome, and there are surely more interesting topics we might discuss."

Lady Catherine's expression darkened momentarily, but then she nodded, seemingly mollified by Mr. Bennet's deference. "Very well," she said. "What do you propose we talk about instead?"

Thomas Bennet smirked, clearly pleased with himself as he leaned back in his chair. "Well, I was thinking we could discuss the merits of a good game of whist," he replied, his voice dripping with sarcasm.

Lady Catherine's eyes narrowed, and Elizabeth held her breath, wondering if her father had gone too far. But to her surprise, Lady Catherine's lips twitched upwards into a small smile.

"Ah, yes, whist," she said, her voice laced with amusement. "I enjoy a good game, for it is yet another endeavor in which I am exceedingly proficient. Perhaps after dinner, when the tables are set, we might make things interesting and play for a wager?"

Elizabeth's eyes widened at the suggestion. She suspected her father had a weakness for gambling from what she had surmised during their talks and feared he might get carried away in the presence of their esteemed guest. But to her relief, her father shook his head, declining the offer.

"I think I shall stick to playing for fun, your ladyship," he said, a twinkle in his eye.

Once the meal had ended and everyone returned to the drawing room, Lady Catherine approached Thomas Bennet. "Mr. Bennet, I trust you are enjoying your visit here at Pemberley despite its being long overdue."

"Long overdue, indeed. But that does not make it any less pleasurable, I assure you."

"I suppose you have a point. No doubt Elizabeth is pleased that you have come."

"I believe she is, your ladyship."

"I understand you have received a letter from Mr. Collins?"

The gentleman raised an eyebrow. "Yes, I have," he replied cautiously. "I was not aware there was a connection between you two."

"Ours is an acquaintance of a short duration but an important one indeed."

"How so, if you do not mind my asking?"

"I am that young man's patroness. Indeed, I am the one who encouraged him to write to you and offer an olive branch. Once he made me aware of the rift in your family owing to the entail on your estate, I felt honor-bound to do so."

"How benevolent of you, Lady Catherine."

"I am sure you and I want what is best for your daughter. I fear her time here in Derbyshire has given her a false impression of what awaits her. The sooner she is away from Pemberley the better for all parties concerned."

Bennet could not help but agree with Lady Catherine, even though it turned his stomach knowing that in taking his daughter away from Pemberley he was, in fact, doing Lady Catherine de Bourgh's bidding.

He forced a polite smile. "I shall certainly keep that in mind, your ladyship. But I trust you understand that my daughter's happiness and well-being are my utmost priority."

"Of course, Mr. Bennet," Lady Catherine said, her tone condescending. "But sometimes, as parents, we must make tough decisions for the sake of our children's future."

Mr. Bennet bristled at her implication but kept his expression neutral. "I understand," he said. "But I believe Elizabeth is more than capable of making her own decisions regarding her future."

Lady Catherine's eyes narrowed. "Let us pray for everyone's sake that your faith in your daughter's good judgment is justified. Else I shall be seriously displeased. Mind you, I am not one to countenance disappointment—particularly when my own child's future is at stake."

"We both want what is best for our only daughters, do we not?"

"Indeed," she said. "Well, I am glad we understand each other, Mr. Bennet. Now, if you will excuse me, I must retire for the evening. Tomorrow promises to be a busy day."

With that, her ladyship swept out of the room, and Mr. Bennet let out a sigh of relief. He could feel Elizabeth's eyes on him, and he turned to her with a wry smile. In a very real sense, he and Lady Catherine de Bourgh were cohorts in separating Elizabeth and the young heir to Pemberley. Even though it was the right thing to do, it still left a sour taste in his mouth.

Chapter 9 - Desperation

ELIZABETH AWOKE with a sense of pride, having observed and admired her father's manner of teasing Lady Catherine the previous evening. Throughout, he wore a knowing smirk and a twinkle in his eye. She could imagine few people handling Lady Catherine with such dignified impertinence, yet her father had accomplished it.

She particularly appreciated his skill in diverting the conversation away from marriage, a subject that even made Lady Catherine's daughter, Anne, uncomfortable. Elizabeth was familiar with Lady Anne and her sister's plans for their children, thanks to Lady Catherine. She could recite the sisters' refrain by heart: the cousins were destined to marry, an obligation and a union meant to unite two great families.

Though Elizabeth could not speak for Anne, she knew Fitzwilliam was not easily influenced by others' desires. While Lady Anne did not discuss the arranged marriage between the cousins as fervently as Lady Catherine, Elizabeth believed she desired it just as much. Lady Anne's comparative silence was evidence of her own yearning whenever the topic arose.

What surprised Elizabeth the most about her father's mockery of Lady Catherine's views on unequal alliances was her suspicion that he shared the same sentiment.

He practically implied as much by insinuating that my supposed infatuation with Fitzwilliam would result in disappointment.

Elizabeth saw her father's intervention as confirmation that if she returned to Hertfordshire with him and met this heir apparent to the estate, perhaps she would not be coerced into an undesired alliance after all.

During a peaceful afternoon stroll, Elizabeth's musings were interrupted by her companion's hurried footsteps. "Miss Elizabeth! You must know—there have been rumors below stairs that

Pemberley's houseguest, your father, is making a spectacle of himself at the gambling establishment in Lambton," she blurted out.

Elizabeth jolted, incredulous. Her dark eyes widened and her heart sank as she realized the gravity of the situation. If word spread about this incident, the Darcy family's reputation would be tarnished by shame.

"Have the Darcys heard? Do they know about this news?" she demanded of the other woman.

Her companion shook her head gravely. "No, I do not believe so," was the reply.

Elizabeth felt a chill run down her spine as she comprehended the magnitude of the situation. The thought of her father being the cause of rumors directed at Pemberley filled her with dread. What if they blamed or even despised her? She did not know what she would do if that happened, yet she could not shake the sense that disaster loomed.

At that moment, she determined to act without delay and set off for Lambton with great tenacity, with her companion following closely behind.

Upon arriving at the public house, Elizabeth found her father in a drunken stupor, surrounded by a rowdy crowd laughing and mocking him. The air was thick with the stench of whiskey, sweat, and tobacco smoke. Overwhelmed with shame and worry for her father, all she wanted was to remove him from the harrowing situation, but her distress rendered her powerless.

Mr. Bennet's countenance was haggard and unkempt. His rumpled clothing and unshaven chin spoke of his disordered state. A glimmer of recognition sparked within him when his bleary eyes fell upon Elizabeth standing by the table.

"Ah, there is my favorite daughter," he said, his voice loud and gruff, brimming with self-importance. "Lizzy, come and sit by my side. I could use a stroke of luck at the moment. The cards, you see, are not my friends."

"Come on, Lizzy!" one of the men barked, slurring his words. "Do you think you can help him out? Considering all he's lost and all..."

Another man interrupted and jeered, "Yeah, perhaps you could show us a bit of hospitality? Make up for what your father lost." They all laughed raucously as they gestured toward Elizabeth with their tankards, their contents carelessly spilling about.

"If your father can't pay his debt," one man

spat, "you'd better have something else we'd be willing to take instead." The others chuckled, reaching out to grab at her as if she were nothing more than an object for them to ogle and smirk at.

It was the worst of times, and Elizabeth had never been treated so cruelly in her life. She tried to persuade her father to leave, but he steadfastly insisted on playing one more hand. As the men taunted and jeered, their words slurred and their gestures menacing, Elizabeth felt anger and fear surge within her. The dimly lit tavern seemed to close in on her, its stale air heavy with the stench of ale and smoke. She could almost taste the bitterness in her mouth, matching the bitter cruelty of the men surrounding her.

The situation continued in that manner until one of the men said, "Come here, you little temptress," flicking a greasy lock of hair from his eyes as he grasped Elizabeth's arm and tried to pull her toward him. The other men laughed and clinked their mugs together, enjoying the cruel spectacle that had unfolded before them.

Elizabeth winced. "Take your hand off me!" she shouted pleadingly, evoking roaring laughter at her feeble attempts. By now, her father was nearly slumped over the table.

The man holding on to Elizabeth drew closer, his breath reeking of ale and his eyes full of lust. "Oh, come now, don't be shy," he said, his hand moving up her arm. "We just want to have a bit of fun."

Elizabeth was overcome with sheer dread and loathing. She knew she had to escape from the dire predicament, but her courage seemed to have abandoned her, leaving her frozen in place.

At that moment, salvation arrived in the form of Fitzwilliam Darcy, pushing his way through the crowd with determined strides. He surveyed the scene with one sweeping glance while Elizabeth stood frozen in fear and revulsion. His muscles tensed, and he struck the drunken man in the jaw in one swift move, freeing Elizabeth from his grasp.

He glared at Mr. Bennet. "I believe you have had enough for one day. Let us return to Pemberley."

"Pemberley? I'll be damned if we let him leave until he pays us what he owes!" the speaker slurred, slamming his mug onto the table and spilling ale.

Bennet waved his hand dismissively. "Do not worry, my friend, because I have no intention of going anywhere with this young man. I am my own man and take orders from no one," he declared defiantly, his speech slurred.

Fitzwilliam turned to Elizabeth. "Come with me. This is no place for a young lady."

"No! I will not leave my father here like this."

"Elizabeth?"

She turned to her father. "Papa, please let us both leave." She glanced over her shoulder. "This dark and filthy room reeks and is no place for either of us."

Mr. Bennet folded his hand. "Very well, my child. Very well."

"Hold your horses, mate!" one of the other players said. "What makes you think you can just take off without paying up? You owe me, and I intend to collect what's rightfully mine."

"My dearest intention is to settle my full debt with you," Mr. Bennet declared as he reached into his pocket, searching for his coin purse. Alas, it was not there. He patted down the other pocket with no better luck. "I fear I have been placed at a considerable disadvantage, for my funds and I seem to have parted ways!"

Hearing this, the men stood up, their anger growing with each passing second as their hostile expressions and menacing murmurs indicated.

"What is his debt?" Fitzwilliam asked.

As the gamblers discussed various sums, Fitzwilliam did not bother waiting for a definitive response. Instead, he retrieved a soft bundle of notes from his pocket and tossed it on the table.

By the look on his face it was impossible to discern whether he was more disgusted by the greedy men or Mr. Bennet. The men fell silent as they gawked at the substantial sum of money before them. Darcy looked each man in the eye, his expression serious. "I trust this is enough to cover the gentleman's debt."

The men nodded, and with that, Fitzwilliam assisted Mr. Bennet in standing upright. With Elizabeth on one side and Fitzwilliam on the other, they departed from the disreputable establishment in as dignified a manner as possible given the circumstances.

Fitzwilliam was livid, and to be honest, some of his anger was directed toward Elizabeth. What had she been thinking going to Lambton alone and putting herself in harm's way? Who knew what might have happened to her if he had not arrived when he did? Her father certainly could not have protected her in his state.

He searched his mind, wondering if he had ever seen any of the men from earlier. Those men were more likely strangers in the area, merely passing through, for they would have recognized Elizabeth if they were familiar with the town. They would have known she was not without protection. Being strangers, they did not know, nor did they care. The thought chilled him realizing what Elizabeth might have experienced, further diminishing his already feeble regard for her irresponsible father.

And this man intends to take Elizabeth to Hertfordshire when he leaves Pemberley.

Initially, Fitzwilliam had believed it was not his place to prevent Elizabeth from going if it was truly what she wanted. However, after the events of that afternoon, he was not so sure.

Thoughts of Elizabeth finding herself in such a place consumed his busy mind. A seedy side was bound to exist even in the quaintest of towns. One just needed to know where to find it. How fortunate that his servant had located him. Not only did he inform Fitzwilliam that Elizabeth had ventured to the disreputable establishment in search of her father, but he also led Darcy there.

Later that same day, Elizabeth went to her father's apartment to check on him. She was concerned about his state of mind and worried he might end up in a similar situation again. She also wanted to know why he had gone to such a deplorable establishment in the first place.

Does he often frequent such places in Hertfordshire?

She found him sleeping soundly, and she could not help but wonder what had led him to this point. Elizabeth felt deeply saddened as she looked at her father's sleeping face and vowed to help him, no matter the cost. She laid a comforting hand on his shoulder. She silently promised never to let him experience such shame and helplessness again.

Not so long as it is in my power to prevent it.

Next, Elizabeth found Fitzwilliam alone in the drawing room, gazing out the window. She approached him and said, "Fitzwilliam, on my father's behalf, thank you for coming to our rescue."

"If you will thank me, let it be on your own behalf, for in acting the way I did, I thought only of you."

She sighed. "I know you do not like my father."

"It does not matter what I think of your father, Elizabeth. You are my first priority, always."

"Please do not tell your parents about any of this. I would not want them to think ill of my father."

"Elizabeth—" Fitzwilliam began then thought better of it. The last thing he wanted was to cause her more pain than she had already endured in one day. Surely she must know that his parents harbored no illusions regarding Mr. Bennet. It was not that they judged him—Fitzwilliam did not believe they did—but he knew his parents well enough to know they were not blind to their old friend's shortcomings. They knew, even if they pretended otherwise.

Chapter 10 - Resignation

Days had come and gone since the fateful incident at the seedy establishment in Lambton. Yet, the tension between Fitzwilliam and Elizabeth lingered thick, like a dense fog. Elizabeth could not shake the feeling that Fitzwilliam was judging her and her father, especially given the way he had looked at her in the aftermath of her reckless disregard for her safety.

She fiddled with her hands, still embarrassed by her father's behavior. Yet, beneath that layer of shame, a fierce protectiveness for her father burned within her. She knew he needed her now more than ever. In the depths of her heart, she convinced herself that this was the true reason he had come to Pemberley in the first place—a desperate plea for her help—he just did not know how to tell her.

She found Fitzwilliam seated at a grand mahogany desk in the library, bathed in the soft glow of sunlight filtering through the tall windows. The room exuded an aura of serenity, the scent of aged leather and polished wood mingling harmoniously.

Lost in a sea of papers and documents, Fitzwilliam presented a figure of focused determination. His chiseled features were accentuated by the play of shadows across his face. His brow was furrowed with intensity, emphasizing the weight of his responsibilities.

His concentration wavered as she approached, and a flicker of surprise danced across his countenance as he looked up and met her gaze.

"Is there something you need, Elizabeth?" he asked, his tone guarded.

"I ... I merely wish to speak with you," Elizabeth said, her voice barely audible as if the solemnity of her thoughts threatened to choke her words.

With a resigned sigh, Fitzwilliam set aside his papers, giving her his undivided attention. "Very well. What would you like to talk about?"

She hated it when he was disappointed with her. "It is about my father," she began, drawing in a deep breath, her voice tinged with trepidation. "I understand that you disapprove of him, but he is in dire need of my care. He is unwell, and he requires someone to watch over him. I must consider returning to Hertfordshire with my father. For me to remain here in Derbyshire would be akin to abandoning him, and I cannot possibly do that to him in his time of need."

A sinking feeling settled within Fitzwilliam's chest at the mention of her leaving. He had grown accustomed to her presence at Pemberley and could not bear the thought of her leaving. "Elizabeth, I understand your concern for your father, but you must also think of yourself. You have a life here, with us—with me. Returning to Hertfordshire should be a choice driven by your desires, not solely by a sense of obligation."

Her shoulders sagged. "I am well aware of all that, Fitzwilliam, but he is still my father. I ... I owe him."

"But Elizabeth, you barely know your father. He has not been a part of your life, and while I commend your desire to take care of him, is it really your responsibility?"

Elizabeth sighed, her shoulders slumping. "I know it is not my responsibility."

His expression softened, a tender warmth replacing the guardedness in his eyes. "I cannot fault your sense of duty, but I worry for your well-being. What will become of you if you relinquish your own aspirations and return to Hertfordshire? Your future shines brightly, brimming with potential. I do not want to see you squander that."

"I do not want to squander my future either," Elizabeth said, raising her head to look at him. "But I cannot ignore my father's needs. I am all he has left."

Fitzwilliam nodded. "I understand. I will not stand in your way. Promise me this, Elizabeth. Promise me that you will delay your decision until I return to Pemberley."

"Where are you going?" Elizabeth asked, her eyes searching his for clues.

"I must travel to the north with my father for business that we can no longer delay," Fitzwilliam said, rising from his chair.

"How long will you be gone?" Elizabeth asked, her worry etched across her features.

Fitzwilliam hesitated, his eyes meeting hers. "I am uncertain, but rest assured I will return as swiftly as I can."

"Please be careful."

A wistful smile touched Fitzwilliam's lips as he reached out, his hand cupping her cheek with tenderness. Oh, how desperately he longed to do more—to bridge the chasm between them, to indulge in the forbidden sweetness of her lips. To have the tension and worry that had enveloped them dissipate beneath the heat of their shared desire. But the unspoken boundaries that governed their relationship held him back, reminding him that now was not the time.

"You have my promise. And what of my request, dearest Elizabeth?" he asked, peering into her eyes. "Do you promise to await my return before making a final decision?"

Elizabeth trembled, the gravity of his demand washing over her. After a lingering pause, she declared firmly, though in scarcely more than a murmur, "I promise."

Fitzwilliam nodded, his eyes conveying a silent understanding that what she had promised was no small thing. "Thank you, Elizabeth," he said softly. Savoring the moment and the nearness of her presence, he leaned in to bestow a lingering albeit chaste kiss on her forehead.

Elizabeth closed her eyes, inhaling deeply and treasuring the warmth of his touch and the tenderness of the moment. When he pulled away, she opened them again, meeting his gaze with an unspoken understanding that even if duty and circumstance forced them apart, destiny had already united them in a lasting and irrevocable bond.

Chapter 11 - Expectation

Elizabeth took a deep breath, steeling herself as she entered Lady Anne's elegant sitting room. The warm glow of the afternoon sun spilled through the tall windows, casting soft rays of light upon the room's plush furnishings and delicate tapestries. Her heart fluttered with a mixture of gratitude and trepidation, for Lady Anne had been a second mother to her, nurturing her with love and care. But now Elizabeth feared that her decision to leave Pemberley would be perceived as a betrayal.

Of all the time spent in that particular room, Elizabeth had never been so anxious.

Lady Anne looked up from her desk, her eyes

gentle yet unreadable, as Elizabeth approached. The scent of lavender filled the air, a soothing fragrance that had always lingered in Lady Anne's presence. "Elizabeth, my dear, it is good to see you. How are you?"

"I am well, thank you," Elizabeth replied, taking a seat opposite Lady Anne. Her fingers nervously traced the intricate patterns etched into the armrest. "I came to talk to you about something important, Lady Anne."

Her ladyship folded her dainty hands, her expression serene. "I am listening," she said, her voice a comforting melody.

Summoning her courage, Elizabeth began by offering her sincere apologies for the scandal caused by her father's recent behavior which by now had widely circulated throughout the halls of Pemberley as well as beyond. "How can I make amends?" she asked earnestly, her eyes fixed on Lady Anne's.

A flicker of understanding, laced with sympathy, graced Lady Anne's countenance. "Surely you must know that I do not hold you accountable for your father's actions," she reassured Elizabeth, her voice carrying a gentle grace. "We all must accept responsibility for our own conduct, and your father is no exception. Please, do not trouble yourself in that regard."

Her throat tight with emotion, Elizabeth swallowed hard. "I have been contemplating returning to Hertfordshire with my father," she confessed.

Lady Anne's eyes widened in surprise, but she quickly composed herself. "I see. And what has brought about this decision?"

The burden of her father's frailties pressed heavily upon Elizabeth's heart, and tears threatened to spill from her eyes. "My father is not well," she said, trembling. "He needs me, Lady Anne. I cannot abandon him in his time of need."

Understanding and empathy flickered in Lady Anne's eyes. "Of course, my dear," she murmured, her voice a balm to Elizabeth's troubled soul. "Your father needs you now more than ever. It is commendable that you are willing to put his needs before your own."

An odd sense of relief washed over Elizabeth. "Still, I cannot help but feel somewhat conflicted. While I spent the first eight years of my life at Longbourn, I have lived here at Pemberley even longer. I have no memories of my own mother, and were it not for you, I would not be the young woman I am today."

"You cannot know how proud I am of you, Elizabeth. You are everything a young woman ought to be—intelligent and fiercely independent. While I should hate to part with you, you must know you will always hold a special place in my heart. Because of you, I have been blessed with rearing a daughter—overseeing her coming out and presentation at court. All the things a mother would wish for a daughter. If I have any regret at all, it is that I shall not be there when you meet and fall in love with a gentleman who is truly worthy of you."

Here, Lady Anne paused and took Elizabeth's hand in hers. "By that, I mean really fall in love," she murmured, her voice carrying a mixture of longing and wisdom. "Not trapped in the fleeting throes of infatuation or other girlish sentiments." Her grasp tightened briefly, conveying unspoken understanding, before she released Elizabeth's hand. "I trust you take my meaning."

Before Elizabeth could fashion a response, Lady Anne said, "As much as I should hate to see you leave Pemberley, I am sure it is for the best for all concerned. As you pursue this next chapter in life, I have no doubt you shall find your own happiness, as I am certain my son, Fitzwilliam, and my niece, Anne, will soon find theirs once he is no longer distracted by other frivolous matters clouding his judgment and making him forget his responsibility to his family."

A sigh escaped Elizabeth's lips. "With all due respect, you and Lady Catherine did as much as you could in planning the union. Surely you will concede that its execution depends solely on others."

"That may very well be the case, Elizabeth. I am not so foolish as to believe that I can actually control whom my son intends to spend his life with. However, as their union has long been my favorite wish, it would undoubtedly break my heart if he were to choose to marry someone other than my niece and namesake, Anne."

Other frivolous matters clouding his judgment. The more Elizabeth reflected on Lady Anne's speech the more she could not help but think those words were a reference to her.

Rather than be disappointed by Elizabeth's

decision to leave, it was as if Lady Anne applauded it. She was certain that were Lady Catherine de Bourgh still at Pemberley, she would be packing Elizabeth's bags for her and shoving her out the door, but Lady Anne? It had always lingered as an unspoken fear within Elizabeth's heart that Lady Anne saw Fitzwilliam's involvement with her as a distraction from his duty to his family and his responsibilities as the future master of Pemberley. She had never wanted to be the cause of any friction between them; she had only wanted, albeit secretly, to love Fitzwilliam with all her heart, secure in the notion that if they were truly meant to be, then nothing would stand in their way.

Her ladyship brokered no disappointment, not when it concerned the family's standing in society. They were a proud people whose roots were steeped in the aristocracy. No, she would never allow her son to marry beneath him, and despite Lady Anne raising and caring for Elizabeth as she would have done for her own daughter, had she lived, Elizabeth was not of noble blood. She was not wealthy in her own right. Therefore she was not deemed worthy of being the next mistress of Pemberley.

The last thing she wanted to do in leaving Pemberley was to cause Lady Anne any pain. Until that moment, it had never once dawned on Elizabeth that her leaving Pemberley would be a cause for anyone's joy.

She pushed the thought from her mind and focused on the task at hand. First, she needed to speak to her father and tell him about her decision. Then she needed to start packing and preparing for the journey back to Hertfordshire. As Lady Anne had aptly insinuated, the sooner they were away the better it would be for all concerned.

As she walked through the halls of Pemberley the next morning to the waiting carriage outside, quite possibly for the last time, she could not help but feel a pang of sadness. This place had been her home for so long and it was hard to imagine leaving it behind. She would miss Pemberley terribly, but she knew she was doing the right thing for her father, the Darcys, and, most importantly, herself.

Part of Elizabeth had wished to avoid Lady Anne, fearing further judgment or disapproval. But when the time came to say goodbye, Lady Anne surprised her.

"Elizabeth, my dear," she said, taking Elizabeth's hands in hers. "I know you must leave us now, but I want you to know that you will always be welcome at Pemberley. This will always be your home, and I will always consider you as akin to a daughter."

Elizabeth was taken aback by Lady Anne's words. She had been so focused on her own concerns that she had forgotten how much Lady Anne truly cared for her, even if she was opposed to Elizabeth's connection to her son.

"Thank you, Lady Anne," she said, tears filling her eyes. "You have been like a mother to me, and I will never forget all you have done for me."

Lady Anne pulled Elizabeth into a fierce embrace, holding her tightly. "Go now, my dear. And know that I will always be proud of you and love you as if you were my own."

Elizabeth pulled away from Lady Anne, feeling a sense of warmth spreading throughout her body. She knew leaving Pemberley would be difficult, but with Lady Anne's blessing, she felt more at ease about her decision.

With a final farewell, Elizabeth and her father climbed into the carriage and watched as Pemberley disappeared from view. It was the end of one chapter in her life, but she knew the future held countless possibilities. She would always cherish the memories she had made at Pemberley, but it was time to turn the page and start a new journey.

Chapter 12 - Deception

LADY ANNE STOOD by the window, looking out as Elizabeth's carriage drew further away, effectively removing temptation from her son, and a part of her wished it did not have to be that way. She loved Elizabeth, and she was sure she would miss her dearly. Perhaps once either of the two young people had married their intended spouses, she would find a way to make amends to Elizabeth for harboring such feelings as she did.

However, for now, this is the only way.

Lady Anne's thoughts were interrupted by a knock at the door. It was the housekeeper, Mrs. Reynolds.

With a graceful curtsy, Mrs. Reynolds addressed her mistress, her voice filled with deference. "Your ladyship, I have something pertaining to Miss Elizabeth that I thought you should see."

Lady Anne's heart skipped a beat, her curiosity piqued. "What is it?"

"It seems that Miss Elizabeth left a letter for Master Fitzwilliam before she departed," Mrs. Reynolds said, holding out a sealed envelope. "I thought you might want to see it."

She extended a sealed envelope toward Lady Anne, who accepted it with a trembling hand. The familiar script on the envelope confirmed it was Elizabeth's handwriting.

"Thank you, Mrs. Reynolds," Lady Anne said, her voice measured. "From now on, any correspondence of this nature is to be brought directly to me. I shall be the only one to pass such correspondence to him, do you understand?" she asked, having emphasized the word *only*.

She, of course, had no intention of sharing any such letters with her son, but the housekeeper did not need to know that. The servants had nothing to do with how she conducted her household affairs. Nor did she intend to let her husband know the means she was employing to place distance between Darcy and Elizabeth. She was only doing what was in everyone's best interest.

Lady Anne had always been a pragmatist. She knew that sometimes difficult decisions must be made for the greater good. And in this case, she believed hiding the truth from her son was the best course of action.

She knew that Fitzwilliam had been distracted lately owing to Mr. Bennet's visit and all that it had entailed, and she feared that if he were to read Elizabeth's letter, it would only serve to further cloud his judgment. Lady Anne had always been a staunch defender of the Darcy family's reputation, and she could not bear the thought of her son making a mistake that could tarnish their name.

If Fitzwilliam believes that Elizabeth has left without saying goodbye, then perhaps he will be able to move on and focus on his responsibilities at Pemberley.

Far better if he believes Elizabeth left Pemberley without even a letter explaining her actions.

On the other hand, she was denying Elizabeth the chance to explain herself. No doubt there was a reason Elizabeth had left without waiting long enough to say goodbye to Fitzwilliam in person, and Lady Anne was not giving her the opportunity to share it. A troubling thought entered her mind. *What if Elizabeth meant to tell my son our conversa-*

tion was a compelling factor in her leaving Pemberley? And if that were the case, would that not be reason enough to withhold the letter from Fitzwilliam?

Lady Anne shook her head. *No, I know Elizabeth too well to suspect she would ever do or say anything that might cause a rift between me and my son.* She placed her hand over her mouth. *But what if Elizabeth's affection for Fitzwilliam supersedes her loyalty to me?*

As she paced the floor, Lady Anne's mind drifted back to her own youth, when she had fancied herself in love with a man whose family was beneath her own in consequence. It had been her duty to form an advantageous alliance that would enhance her family's fortunes, not burden them with the derision that comes with an unequal alliance, and if she were lucky enough to love her future husband half as much as she fancied herself in love with first love, then all the better. Time and distance from her first love taught her that what she felt for him was never really love but a girlish infatuation.

No doubt, Elizabeth is facing a similar situation, her ladyship concluded. Lady Anne could see the affection in Elizabeth's eyes whenever she looked at Fitzwilliam. Still, she also knew that their connection was not without its complications. Elizabeth was not of their social standing, and many would never accept her as a suitable match for Fitzwilliam, Lady Anne being among the greatest detractors second to her sister, Lady Catherine.

Her ladyship took a deep breath and steeled herself for the decision she was about to make. She would keep the letter from her son for now, but she would read it herself and find out what Elizabeth had to say. It was the only way she could ensure that her family's reputation remained intact and that her son was protected from his misguided inclinations where Elizabeth was concerned.

She shook her head to clear her thoughts and took the letter to her private chambers. She set it on her writing desk and sat down to contemplate her next move. She knew that she had to open the letter, but she also knew that doing so would be a breach of Elizabeth's trust. Lady Anne closed her eyes for a moment and took a deep breath.

With trembling hands, she broke the envelope seal and unfolded the letter. Elizabeth's handwriting was neat and precise, and Lady Anne felt a pang of sadness as she recalled the many letters she had helped Elizabeth write to her father when she was younger. After a moment or two, her ladyship commenced reading.

"My dearest Fitzwilliam," Elizabeth had written. *"I cannot bear the thought of leaving you, but I know it is..."*

Lady Anne gasped at this version of herself and hastily folded Elizabeth's missive. She could not bear to read any more of it. The guilt of violating Elizabeth's trust was too much to bear. She sat there for a moment, feeling the weight of her actions pressing down on her.

But she also knew her duty was to protect her son's future, no matter the cost. She tucked the letter into her pocket, determined to keep it safe until she could find a way to dispose of it without causing more harm than necessary.

Chapter 13 - Separation

Fitzwilliam Darcy and his father had just returned from their business trip to the north, their weary faces bearing the telltale signs of their travels, when they were met by Lady Anne in the grand foyer of Pemberley. Fitzwilliam immediately noticed the distress etched upon her face, a sight that clenched his heart with worry.

"Mother, what is the matter?" he asked, his voice laced with concern, his tall figure towering over her petite frame.

"Elizabeth has gone," Lady Anne said. "She left Pemberley with her father earlier today."

Fitzwilliam's heart sank at the news. He had been looking forward to seeing Elizabeth again, but now it seemed that opportunity had been snatched from him.

"Why did she leave?" he asked, trying to hide the pain in his voice.

Lady Anne hesitated briefly before responding, her expression fraught with unspoken worries. The three of them having moved their discussion to the drawing room, as Fitzwilliam listened to his mother's words, panic surged within him. Elizabeth had departed without a word, contradicting her promise to await his return before making any final decisions. It was uncharacteristic of her to break such a promise, leaving him to wonder if some untoward event had transpired during his absence, something that could explain her sudden and impulsive departure. The possibilities raced through his mind, but none offered a satisfactory explanation.

"I cannot fathom why Elizabeth would leave without providing a reason. Did she give you an explanation? Did something happen while I was away?" he asked, his voice tight with emotions he struggled to contain.

"Nothing out of the ordinary. Elizabeth sought me out to inform me she was returning to Hertfordshire with her father."

"Did she say more?"

Lady Anne shook her head solemnly. "I am afraid not, Fitzwilliam."

Fitzwilliam's heart sank further. Even if Elizabeth was bound and determined to leave Pemberley, he thought certainly he would have had more time with her before she left.

"I do not understand," he said, shaking his head. "Why would she leave without saying goodbye to me?"

"I think it is best that we do not dwell on the reasons for her leave-taking," she said, choosing her words carefully. "Suffice it to say that Elizabeth has returned to Hertfordshire with her father. Perhaps it is best she puts some distance between herself and Pemberley for a time."

Fitzwilliam felt a knot form in his stomach. "How can you say such a thing when you know Pemberley is more of a home to her than Longbourn in Hertfordshire?"

His voice calm and authoritative, Mr. Darcy said, "Son, you have known for some time that Mr. Bennet intended to persuade Elizabeth to return with him. As her father, he had every right to expect her compliance."

"There is more to being a father than siring a

child," Fitzwilliam said. The picture of Mr. Bennet in the seedy establishment in Lambton flashed in his mind. To know that Elizabeth was traveling so far away with her only protection being a neglectful, irresponsible man she barely knew was too much to bear. He consulted his watch. "Perhaps if I make haste, I can intercept their carriage."

"Assuming you meet with success, what do you plan to do, Son? Surely you do not mean to persuade her to return to Pemberley. Deciding to leave could not have been easy. What is done is done."

"I do not plan to cause her to second-guess her decision, but I owe it to her to accompany her and ensure her safe passage."

A chord of panic crossed Lady Anne's features. "I declare you will do no such thing!"

"Surely you cannot expect me to stand idly by and do nothing!"

"I do not expect you to make a fool of yourself either. Besides, she is not without protection. Her father is accompanying her. He is Elizabeth's protector, Son. Not you." Lady Anne explained that the Bennets had not opted for public transportation but were traveling in one of the Darcys' carriages with all that such an arrangement entailed.

Fitzwilliam found a glimmer of solace in the thought, yet it was offset by the image of Elizabeth traveling so far without the safeguard that he had convinced himself only he could provide. It tore away at his equanimity.

"He cannot protect Elizabeth! He does not even know her."

"If you care as much for Elizabeth as you espouse, and I have no doubt you do, then you must teach yourself to respect her decision. Besides, there are far more consequential matters for you to concern yourself with, my son."

"What can be more consequential to me than Elizabeth's well-being, Mother?"

"Why! Your obligation to your family. Use this time to remember who you are and what you are about."

Fuming, Fitzwilliam said, "This is no time for you to remind me of my so-called obligation to marry my cousin."

"I will not have you speak so dismissively about your engagement to Anne. If you must travel, then go to Matlock instead."

"Matlock?" both gentlemen cried out in unison.

"Yes. My sister and Anne have returned to Matlock, having concluded their travels further north, where they shall remain for the rest of the month. Go there yourself and use the time to get better acquainted with your cousin. This will be your first opportunity to spend time with Anne outside of Elizabeth's presence in years."

Fitzwilliam brushed both hands over his face and released a heavy sigh. He looked at his father. "Is this your opinion as well?"

The older man shook his head. "You already know my opinion on the subject, Son."

Whereas the elder man was not so firm in the general regard that his only son was to marry his wealthy cousin Miss Anne de Bourgh, it was absolutely incumbent upon his son to choose a wife with her own fortune. He believed one's family could never have too much of what was good for them, and what could possibly be better than extensive property and an abundance of wealth? The gentleman's sentiment might have been rather harsh, but what of it? People of the Darcys' ilk were wealthy and powerful for a reason. Every generation of Darcys from as far back as the older man could remember had played its part in their current standing in Derbyshire, be it through increased wealth, heightened social standing, or both, and he did not mean for all that to end with his own son.

What a shame, too, for Gerald Darcy loved Elizabeth as much as he would have loved his own daughter, of that he was convinced. He enjoyed a healthy respect for his friend Thomas Bennet as well. Being with her own father at that point in their lives was the right thing for everyone—for the father and daughter whose bond was desperately in want of repair and for Fitzwilliam and Elizabeth, who were far too attached to each other for two people whose lives, despite their having been reared under the same roof, in truth, were worlds apart.

Lady Anne was about to fashion a protest against his lack of support for an alliance between Anne and her son, but her husband silenced her with a glance. He continued, "However, I must concur with your mother as regards your following Elizabeth, intending to accompany her to Hertfordshire. Bennet and I had a lengthy discussion the last time we spoke, and he promised me he would do everything in his power to make amends to his daughter. I, for one, trust him, and I shall not countenance your undermining him. He and Elizabeth deserve all of our support, not our interference."

"Father—"

The thought of injuring his son after the heartbreak he suffered as a result of Elizabeth's abrupt departure was the last thing the older man wanted.

"Enough, Fitzwilliam," Mr. Darcy said firmly, cutting off any further argument. "No one forced Elizabeth into this decision I am sure. I strongly advise you to honor her wishes. In time, you might go to Hertfordshire and see her, but for now, she should be allowed to return to her father's home, preside over her father's table, and accustom herself to the sphere in which she was born."

Fitzwilliam knew better than to argue further with his father. He nodded, feeling a mixture of frustration and resignation. He knew his parents meant well and had his best interests at heart, but he could not help but feel they did not understand the depth of his feelings for Elizabeth. He stood up from his seat and made his way toward the door.

"I will leave for Matlock tomorrow morning," he said before turning back to face his parents. "But I cannot promise my heart will be in it."

With that, he left the room, his mind racing with thoughts of Elizabeth and her well-being. He knew he should not interfere, but that did not stop him from worrying about her safety and happiness.

Standing just outside the door, he heard Lady Anne's disapproving sigh and his father saying, "I would not worry about our son, my dear. He will come to see reason in time. For now, we must trust his good judgment and faith in Elizabeth's decisions. She is a strong and capable young woman, and I have no doubt that she will make the best choices for herself."

Fitzwilliam's heart sank as he listened to his father's words. He knew they were right, but it did not make accepting it any easier. He loved Elizabeth with all of his heart, and the thought of being away from her for even a moment filled him with despair.

Elizabeth was gone, and that was that. Any thought he entertained of going after her was quickly dismissed as the wrong thing to do. No one had forced Elizabeth to leave Pemberley; she decided of her own free will, and thus he must live with that decision. Not that Fitzwilliam was surrendering. No, the battle had just begun, for there were other factors that went into play contributing to Elizabeth leaving, even if she never voiced her complaints.

How many times did she have to endure my mother's matchmaking antics, not just in my case but in her case as well?

Just before Mr. Bennet's arrival, his mother had been planning for Elizabeth's second season, where she might thrust her into the marriage market again.

Why would she do such a thing if she did not mean for Elizabeth to meet and fall in love or make an advantageous match with anyone other than me?

Darcy's mind drifted back to the days of his separation from Elizabeth some years ago when they had been torn apart by circumstance. The memories of that time echoed within him, intertwining with his current suffering.

After many months of being apart, he had desperately wanted to see Elizabeth. However, the painful heart-aching sense of wanting her and not having her was taking its toll on his equanimity. Something had to be done. He was not quite sure how to describe the feelings he suffered toward her.

In his heart, he knew that Elizabeth was the most important person in the world to him. He recognized that such an all-encompassing devotion should not be the case for a young man of his age and social standing. He was meant to explore the world, engage in youthful exploits, and expand his circle of acquaintances. There were adventures to be had, both wild and mundane, that he had yet to experience. He had envisioned sharing those moments with Elizabeth, but she, four years his junior, deserved her own share of youthful follies. She should revel in the grandeur of court presentations, the excitement of London's social scene, and all the delights life had to offer before settling into marriage.

He could deny her none of those things. He would not. He had stayed away from Pemberley at Christmas to ease the longing they suffered for each other, but instead of easing them, it only made him miss her more. And he missed her every day that he had spent in London, at White's and on Bond Street and anywhere else where he and his friends congregated and cavorted and lived like the carefree gentlemen of fortune they were. And though he could not imagine meeting and falling in love with a young lady who proved handsome enough to tempt him, who was to say he might not?

The time away from Elizabeth had not served its purpose. His father had written to him of Elizabeth's general malaise—even his mother had hinted at Elizabeth's low spirits. Though his parents did not always venture to town so early in the year, that year would be different. No plans were underway to bring Elizabeth out into society, but there were other diversions to be had.

And so it was decided. He would be there too. He would see Elizabeth. And he would have to get used to being with her even if he was barred from expressing his true feelings for her. What a strange, strange feeling. The thought of her growing up, learning the lessons of society, having seasons, receiving suitors, receiving proposals, and possibly marrying another man...

If only she were older already, he recalled thinking at the time. If only she had already experienced all those things in life that she was meant to enjoy. But all he could do was bide his time, suffer in silence, and wait for her.

. . .

Once again, he resolved to bide his time and give Elizabeth a chance to repair the broken familial bonds with her father and the rest of her Hertfordshire relations.

In the interim, I will let my mother know once and for all to abandon her foolish hopes for an alliance between Anne and me. I will clear the path of any impediment between the future life I wish to have with Elizabeth, and then I shall ask her to be my wife.

For now, I know I must let her go, he silently considered, even though he knew that was easier said than done.

Chapter 14 - Exploration

LONGBOURN IN HERTFORDSHIRE

Elizabeth's steps faltered as her eyes drifted along the corridors of Longbourn. She pushed open the door to the east parlor, and what she saw took her breath away. She stepped into the room. Everything was covered in large, white cloths. She carefully walked around the room, observing with a discerning eye. As she looked closer, she noticed small spider webs in between the furniture and on the edges of the frames that hung on the walls. Even more peculiarly, these, too, were cloaked in white cloth, as if someone purposely hid something mysterious from sight. It was a sight she had never witnessed before, leaving her both bewildered and captivated.

Silence enveloped her as she stood in the stillness, the only sound the ticking of a forgotten clock. Curiosity bubbled within her—wanting to satisfy her inquisitive nature, she had to know what secrets were hidden behind the cloth-covered pictures on the wall. Her hand trembled as she reached for one of them and slowly pulled the covering away. Elizabeth was pleased to discover it was a painting of Longbourn Village depicted from a distance in all its glory. Once again, she was breathless, having no recollection of ever having seen the estate from that particular vantage point. Eyes wide with wonder, she studied every detail—every stroke of color, every brush of light—marveling at how beautifully it captured her father's home—her home.

Does such a prospect really exist or did the artist take liberties in his work?

Her heart quickened at the thought of exploring further, determined to discover the vantage point that had inspired such exquisite artistry during one of her solitary rambles.

Uncertainty tinged her excitement as she uncovered the next frame with trembling hands.

She stared at the canvas and her heart skipped a beat. It was a portrait of her family—a moment frozen in time. The beautiful eyes of her mother, whose image had grown faint in her memories over the years, were shining with warmth and love beside the figure of her father, tall and handsome, right in the prime of his life. On one side stood an adorable little girl with long golden locks and an angelic countenance. In her mother's lap sat young Elizabeth beaming with happiness.

Emotion constricted Elizabeth's chest, and the torrent of tears streaming down her face were a symbol of all the pain and joy that came with the memories locked away in her mind. With each brushstroke of the painting, memories of Jane, her earliest childhood companion, along with the memories of her parents, flooded her senses. She felt the warmth of a summer's day when they all gathered for dinner around the table and heard their laughter echoing through time. The bittersweetness of being able to relive these moments while simultaneously knowing they were now gone forever made Elizabeth sob even more.

Why was the painting covered? she asked herself.

A ray of light shone inside the room, coming from the doorway, but Elizabeth barely flinched as she remained transfixed on the haunting painting. She could vaguely hear the creaking steps of someone entering, but it felt distant and unimportant. She never tore her eyes away from the painting. "Why is everything in this room covered? The furniture, even the paintings on the wall?"

"Madam, I am afraid it was done for the best."

"The best?" Elizabeth repeated, turning in the direction of the speaker, Mrs. Hill, Longbourn's housekeeper, who had uttered the confounding words. "The best for who?" she asked.

True, Longbourn Manor was rather large for a single occupant with so few servants, but was that a sufficient excuse to hide what Elizabeth likened to the heart of the home? Who was to say how many other treasures were hidden therein?

"The best for the master, I am sorry to say. He would often find himself in this room for long hours at a time, the aftermath of which always ended very badly. I dare not say more out of respect for your father's privacy."

Her voice raised and her brow furrowed with confusion and frustration, Elizabeth asked, "If I do not learn what my father did or how he comported himself from you, a most trusted servant, then to whom should I listen?"

"Suffice it to say that when this likeness of your family was captured, your excellent father was very different from the man he is now."

"You seem to suggest spending time in this room had an adverse effect on him."

"Everyone handles grief in their own way. Spending lengthy time in this room always led to his doing things—acting and behaving in ways he otherwise would not," Mrs. Hill said. "I dare not say more."

Whatever the housekeeper would not venture to say gave Elizabeth pause, and she supposed the woman had her reasons. Perhaps it was too painful a recollection to summon; like the pictures and the furniture, the servant's memories that had attached to that room had also been covered, hidden away.

Elizabeth was not too naive to know how hard her mother's and sister's deaths had been on her father. Unlike Elizabeth, who had never set foot inside Longbourn in the wake of her family members' passings, her father had to live with his grief inside the halls of Longbourn every day of his life for the past decade. Not that his sadness could excuse his drinking, gambling, and reckless disregard for his station in life, but as

Mrs. Hill said, everyone dealt with grief in their own way.

Elizabeth hesitated for a moment, not wanting to ask the housekeeper to rehash a painful part of her past. Swallowing the lump in her throat, she wiped away her tears. Her voice was quiet but strong as she spoke. "I want this room restored to its former glory. No part of Longbourn is to remain hidden any longer."

A stunned pause filled the air as the old woman considered Elizabeth's words. Eventually, she mustered up enough courage to ask, "But what of your father?"

With an unwavering resolve, Elizabeth said, "I am here now. I shall bear the responsibility for my father's fate."

Chapter 15 - Observation

ELIZABETH ASSUMED the role of mistress of Longbourn and also that of its steward. Her father kept a small household staff consisting of four people—an elderly couple, Mr. Evan Hill and his wife, the aforementioned Mrs. Hilda Hill, a cook, and a scullery maid. A quick perusal of Mr. Bennet's ledgers indicated that Elizabeth would have to work with this staff until she could improve the estate's management.

Elizabeth's desire to transform Longbourn into a functioning estate arose from her dissatisfaction with its current near-squalor conditions. She refused to adopt her father's indifference toward estate management. Although the property was entailed away from the male line, destined for a virtual stranger upon her father's demise, it remained her birthright for the time being. There was still a possibility that her father might remarry and have a son, which could alter the situation entirely. The realm of possibilities extended at least for the next decade or so.

She contemplated how her father's life might have unfolded differently had he remarried and had more children. A decade had passed, yet Longbourn Village still bore the scars of mourning.

Elizabeth's attempts to engage her father's interest in the estate proved futile. It seemed to be against his nature, and she wondered if it had ever been different. Her suspicions grew when she discovered that Mr. Hill, despite lacking formal education, fulfilled multiple roles as a butler, valet, groomsman, overseer, and steward. He took on numerous responsibilities to the best of his ability.

Mr. Bennet sought solace in his library—a room adorned with books, stacks covering the floors, the chairs, and a cluttered desk. The disorder reflected the life of a recluse who found solace in reading rather than the company of others.

His reputation as a recluse provided Elizabeth

with respite from constant visitors during her initial days at Longbourn. The exception to this was Miss Charlotte Lucas, a young woman from the neighboring estate of Lucas Lodge. Being more than six years Elizabeth's senior, she had maintained a favorable impression of Elizabeth and her late sister and was eager to be of service in smoothing Elizabeth's homecoming. Charlotte's mature and composed demeanor immediately captivated Elizabeth. The effortless flow of their conversation revealed mutual interests, subtly weaving an unspoken bond that she instinctively appreciated.

Also, within the quaint confines of Meryton, a stone's throw away from Longbourn, resided Elizabeth's aunt, Mrs. Phillips, with her husband, Mr. Phillips. As the sibling of Elizabeth's late mother, Mrs. Phillips deemed it her duty to capture a portion of Elizabeth's attention. Amid deflecting the probing questions from curious friends and inquisitive acquaintances craving an insight into the past decade of Elizabeth's life, Mrs. Phillips disrupted Elizabeth's cherished solitude at Longbourn. Her well-intentioned meddling came in the form of an elaborate dinner party thrown in Elizabeth's honor, with a guest list featuring most of the more prominent families.

This social event ensured that Elizabeth's quietude would be disturbed by a relentless succession of intrigued visitors henceforth. However, her companion Charlotte proved to be a saving grace amidst this chaos, deftly guiding her through the web of societal norms, identifying who was worth her time and whom to elude.

As the evening progressed, Elizabeth could not help but feel grateful for Charlotte's companionship. Charlotte's calm and collected demeanor kept her at ease despite the overwhelming crowd. Elizabeth wondered how her friend managed to navigate the social maze with such ease.

"Charlotte, I must express my amazement at your familiarity with everyone here. How did you become so well-regarded?" Elizabeth asked, genuinely intrigued.

Charlotte offered a wry smile. "My dear Elizabeth, popularity is not something I strive for. It is merely a consequence of my father's connections in the community. As my parents have been away from this part of the county since your arrival, you have yet to renew your acquaintance with them. You will understand once you meet Sir William and my mother, Lady Lucas. My mother considers herself quite the social butterfly, thanks to my father's recently elevated rank."

Impressed, Elizabeth nodded. "Yet, you genuinely attract the favor of everyone. It cannot solely be attributed to your father's status."

Charlotte shrugged nonchalantly. "Perhaps it is because I do not seek to impress anyone. I am content with being who I am and do not feel the need to put on airs or graces. People appreciate honesty and simplicity, and that is what I strive to embody."

Elizabeth smiled, sensing a kindred spirit in Charlotte. Her sheltered life in Derbyshire had not afforded such opportunities for female companionship, making her newfound friendship all the more welcome.

"Your philosophy is refreshing, Charlotte," Elizabeth continued, her eyes reflecting the flickering candlelight. "In a society where pretense often overshadows substance, your approach is indeed a breath of fresh air."

Charlotte gave a humble nod. "One learns with time, Elizabeth. But tell me," she cried, "how have you been finding the evening? I hope the onslaught of the whole of Meryton's curiosity is not proving too arduous."

Shrugging, Elizabeth chuckled lightly. "It is no less than I expected. Still," she hesitated, casting a glance at the crowd, "it feels rather peculiar to be the object of such unabashed curiosity. I dread the looming onslaught of callers at Longbourn following this evening's gathering. That is to say nothing of my father's ensuing displeasure."

Charlotte patted her hand sympathetically. "I understand your concerns, Elizabeth. However, rest assured, these curiosities will wane with time. Until then, consider me your faithful guide in this bewildering social dance."

Elizabeth offered her friend a grateful smile. "I have no doubt, dear Charlotte, that this maze will soon feel less daunting with each passing day."

As they shared a moment of comfortable silence, the echo of laughter and soft music from the corner piano filled the space around them. Elizabeth glanced across the sea of faces, catching sight of her well-meaning aunt Mrs. Phillips beaming at her from across the room. With a warm smile, Elizabeth nodded slightly, acknowledging the support she was beginning to appreciate, despite its overwhelming nature.

I have not merely returned to a family eager to stand by my side in this new chapter of life but also a most unexpected gift—the treasure of an intimate friendship with Charlotte that I will surely hold close to my heart.

Chapter 16 - Relations

Mr. Edward Gardiner and his wife, Mrs. Madeline Gardiner, were Longbourn's first official houseguests. The former, Elizabeth's late mother's brother, brought back faint memories due to his jovial nature. However, Elizabeth had never met his wife, as he was unmarried when they last saw each other.

In contrast to her mother's sister, Mrs. Phillips, Mr. Gardiner appeared to possess both sense and education; his wife, too, exhibited intelligence, good taste, and keen sensibilities. The Gardiners were the kind of people Elizabeth could proudly claim as kin. One could easily mistake them for members of the landed gentry, but the truth was that they resided in Cheapside, within sight of their warehouses. Elizabeth gleaned this information from a conversation her father had with the guests.

As they settled into their seats, Elizabeth experienced a sense of contentment as she sipped her tea and engaged in conversation. Having guests in the house provided a welcome change from the usual company of her father and the servants.

When it became apparent that the gentlemen's discussion was shifting toward business matters, Mrs. Gardiner turned her attention to Elizabeth.

"Lizzy," the other woman began tentatively. "I hope it is not inappropriate for me to address you by that name. Or would you prefer I use your given name?"

"Indeed, you may address me however you prefer," Elizabeth replied. She had been called by her given name for years, but upon meeting her father and hearing him call her "Lizzy," a sense of familiarity and comfort had developed.

"Excellent!" exclaimed Mrs. Gardiner. "I much prefer 'Lizzy.' That is how your uncle referred to you when he learned your father was bringing you home to live with him here at Longbourn. If it is

SIMPLY BEAUTIFUL

not too forward of me, may I request a tour of the house? I am fascinated by the interiors of country estates, and Longbourn is no exception. I have heard that the manor house has undergone significant improvements since your return."

Elizabeth gladly agreed, and as they strolled through the halls, Mrs. Gardiner examined every detail with a keen eye. Elizabeth could not help but feel a sense of pride as she showcased the well-appointed rooms and furnishings. It was not Pemberley, but being accustomed to a more refined lifestyle, Elizabeth had made the best of the resources available to her.

Upon entering the east parlor, Mrs. Gardiner paused and turned to Elizabeth with a smile. "My dear, this room is positively divine. The furnishings are exquisite, and the decor is simply lovely." She ventured further into the room. "I love what you have done here, Lizzy. The last time your uncle and I visited your father—or rather, the only time, for there was just one occasion—this room was nothing like it is now."

"I assume you are referring to the furniture, the paintings draped with cloth, and the general neglect," Elizabeth remarked.

"Indeed, but that was a different time. Now

there is warmth in this room, evidence of a woman's touch, if you will." The older woman blushed slightly. "Pray, I hope I have not spoken out of turn."

"No, not at all," Elizabeth assured her. "I understand this was my mother's favorite room in the entire house, and she spent considerable time within these four walls. I felt the same as you do now when I returned and saw how much the room yearned for a woman's touch to restore it to its former glory."

"You have certainly made the most of your time since returning to Longbourn, both inside the manor house and about the grounds," Mrs. Gardiner praised.

"I take no credit for the grounds. After much cajoling on my part, my father has taken the lead in that regard, I am happy to say. The work has brought a much-needed restoration to his spirits. As for the manor house, it may not compare to Pemberley, but it is a comfortable place nonetheless."

Mrs. Gardiner nodded in agreement. "Indeed, it is a comfortable place. But do not underestimate your efforts, Lizzy. You have done a marvelous job with the interiors. As I mentioned, it is a welcome change from our last visit. Your mother would be proud of how you have restored this room to its present state."

Elizabeth felt a lump forming in her throat at the mention of her mother. Having spent most of her life in Derbyshire, she had almost forgotten how much she missed her mother and sister. Returning to Longbourn had reawakened the void in her heart caused by their deaths. She longed for their presence and often wondered how different her life would have been if her mother had been there to offer guidance.

"I miss her every day," she whispered, her voice barely audible.

"I know you do, my dear," Mrs. Gardiner said, placing a comforting hand on Elizabeth's arm. "But she would be so proud of you. You have grown into a fine young woman. You are doing a wonderful job managing this household and caring for your father. I have no doubt that your mother is looking down on you with immense pride."

Touched by Mrs. Gardiner's words, Elizabeth weakly smiled and said, "Thank you."

Mrs. Gardiner smiled warmly and gently squeezed Elizabeth's arm before releasing it. "Now, what say you we continue our tour of the house? I am quite eager to see what other surprises are in store."

Elizabeth nodded gratefully, thankful for the distraction from her thoughts. Together, they resumed their exploration, with Mrs. Gardiner's excitement and enthusiasm proving infectious. Elizabeth found herself enjoying the tour more than she had anticipated. By the time they finished, she felt a sense of comfort in Mrs. Gardiner's company.

As they made their way back to the east parlor, Elizabeth could not help but wonder what it would be like to have a mother figure in her life again—a confidante to seek guidance from. While she supposed she could always turn to Mrs. Gardiner, it was not the same as having her own mother.

As if sensing Elizabeth's thoughts, Mrs. Gardiner turned to her niece with a soft smile. "You know, Lizzy, I may not be your mother, but I am here for you if you ever need someone to talk to. I understand it is not quite the same, but I hope you will consider me a trusted friend."

A familiar lump formed in Elizabeth's throat at the kindness in Mrs. Gardiner's words. "Thank you," she said, her voice filled with emotion.

Mrs. Gardiner smiled warmly. "Now, let us sit and enjoy some tea. My husband and your father will be engrossed in their business talk for some time, so we might as well make the most of our time together."

Elizabeth nodded, grateful for the company. As they settled into their seats, she found solace in Mrs. Gardiner's presence. Perhaps she had found the mother figure she had been missing after all.

Someone who accepts me unconditionally for who I am rather than deems me wanting for who I am not.

If only the arrival of Longbourn's next houseguest provided Elizabeth with even a modicum of the pleasure she had experienced during the Gardiners' visit. Alas, the guest was none other than her distant cousin, Mr. William Collins, who arrived on the very day after the Gardiners had departed.

As Elizabeth observed the carriage pulling up to the front door of Longbourn, surprise washed over her. Lost in the comfort of the company of sensible and refined individuals for the past few days, she had completely forgotten about Mr. Collins' impending arrival.

Mr. Collins, a young man of five and twenty, possessed an unremarkable but tolerable demeanor. Standing at an average height, his frame was of average build, neither particularly slender nor imposingly broad. His face, structured symmetrically, bore features that could best be described as acceptable rather than striking. Heavy-lidded eyes lent an air of seriousness to his countenance, though it was overshadowed by an ingratiating smile that seemed permanently affixed to his lips.

It was evident that Mr. Collins held his appearance in high regard. His careful grooming and subtle display of fashion spoke of a man aspiring to command respect and admiration. Alas, one could not help but suspect that his earnest efforts might yield, at best, a mixture of mirthful amusement and compassionate pity from those who observed him.

Elizabeth greeted him politely, albeit reservedly, as she took in his presence. She was not long in his company before discerning that she was not particularly fond of the gentleman. He was pompous and arrogant and constantly talked about his noble patroness, Lady Catherine de Bourgh. Every mention of that woman's name was akin to a stake being driven into Elizabeth's heart. It was as if he was completely oblivious to the fact that her connection to his haughty patroness was of far longer duration than his own. The only thing that prevented Elizabeth from informing him was her fear that he might never stop singing her ladyship's praises if he knew. And then what would she do? The newcomer did not seem like the sort of person who reveled in his own company. No doubt, he would always be underfoot.

But as a distant cousin, a guest in her father's home, and, just as importantly, the heir apparent to the Longbourn estate, it was her duty to put up with him and make him feel welcome. Elizabeth tried to put on a good face, but she could not help feeling a sense of dread at the thought of spending time with him. Her father was no help, having left her to deal with the guest soon after his arrival.

She knew the gentleman had come to Longbourn intending to offer her his hand in marriage.

To his way of thinking, such an arrangement would undo the damage of the entail on the estate away from the female line of the family. He saw it as a simple solution—she needed a husband, and he needed a wife. Elizabeth's general suspicion that her father was not wholly opposed to such a convenient sentiment made matters worse.

During dinner that evening, Mr. Collins launched into a lengthy speech about the virtues of humility and the importance of obedience to superiors, his fervor bordering on the deranged. He even went so far as to suggest reading Fordyce's sermons to them after the meal. Elizabeth tried her best to listen politely, but her mind kept wandering, thinking of ways to escape the tedious conversation. She yearned for some respite from the insufferable droning yet felt she owed it to her father to stay put, even if it was against her will.

Just when Elizabeth thought she could not take it anymore, Mr. Collins turned to her with a smile. "I must say, Cousin Elizabeth, you look positively radiant this evening. The color of your dress perfectly complements the hue of your eyes."

The compliment took Elizabeth aback. She was not expecting such a kind remark from Mr.

Collins, even though she supposed it was the result of a lengthy rehearsal on his part. "Thank you, Mr. Collins," she said, trying to suppress a smirk from etching across her lips.

She felt her temper flare as her father sat there, his eyes twinkling with delight, his mouth curving into a smirk. It almost seemed he was enjoying the spectacle a little too much.

Mr. Collins continued to praise Elizabeth throughout the meal. While she still found him insufferable, she could not help feeling an odd sense of pleasure at his compliments. At least he was putting forth the effort, even though she was absolutely certain his diligent work was entirely in vain.

The rest of the meal passed in a blur, with Mr. Collins continuing to speak at length about his patroness and his future plans for the Longbourn estate. Elizabeth struggled to maintain her composure, her mind racing with thoughts of escape. She could not bear the thought of spending another minute in Mr. Collins' company, let alone the rest of her life.

As soon as the arduous meal drew to a close, Elizabeth yearned to escape from the suffocating presence of Mr. Collins. She discreetly excused herself from the table, citing a persistent headache as her reason for retiring early. Leaving her father to the company of their obtrusive guest felt justified, given the evening's trials and her father's evident delight in witnessing her struggle.

Relief washed over Elizabeth as she ascended the stairs, her steps light with anticipation of the solitude her room would offer. The door swung open, granting her sanctuary from the social obligations that weighed heavily upon her. Yet, even within the sanctuary of her own chamber, she could not shed the lingering dread that had taken root since Mr. Collins' arrival.

Seated before her dressing table, Elizabeth picked up the ivory-handled brush. She began rhythmically drawing it through her dark tresses, attempting to bring order to her hair and racing thoughts. Just as a semblance of tranquility settled upon her, a soft yet insistent knock echoed through the room, interrupting her respite.

Summoning a measure of composure, she called out, "Come in," her voice betraying the wariness that clung to her like a shroud. A flicker of apprehension crept through her as she pondered whether Mr. Collins, buoyed by his elevated sense of self-importance as the future owner of Longbourn, had taken the audacious liberty of intruding upon her privacy.

To her immense relief, it was not the detestable cousin who crossed the threshold but the housekeeper, Mrs. Hill, her face adorned with a kind and caring smile. The genuine concern etched upon her features brought a fleeting moment of solace to Elizabeth's troubled heart.

"Good evening, madam," Mrs. Hill greeted her, her voice gentle. "I just wanted to make sure you were all right. You seemed quite pale at dinner."

Elizabeth mustered a semblance of gratitude, forcing a smile upon her lips. "I am fine, thank you," she replied, striving to convey a sense of normalcy. "I am tired, I suppose."

Sympathy sparkled in Mrs. Hill's eyes, mirroring the genuine compassion in her voice. "Well, if you need anything, do not hesitate to ask. I am here to help in any way I can."

"Thank you, Mrs. Hill," Elizabeth said, touched by the woman's genuine concern.

As Mrs. Hill retreated from the room, Elizabeth could not help feeling grateful for the housekeeper's kindness. It was moments like these when she keenly felt her mother's absence since her return to Longbourn.

Despite my father's good intentions of ensuring my well-being in our ancestral home, I am certain my mother would never have entertained the nonsensical notion of an alliance between the likes of that ridiculous Mr. Collins and me.

Chapter 17 - Connection

Elizabeth attended a dinner party at the Phillips' home with her companion, Mrs. Eastman, and the ever-present Mr. Collins in tow. She was the recipient of much attention from those among the crowd who were not yet immune to the circumstances of Elizabeth's past—the misfortunes as well as the good fortune of being reared at Pemberley, which was said to be one of the finest estates in Derbyshire.

Yearning for a respite from Mr. Collins' incessant chatter and his declared intention to remain by her side throughout the evening, Elizabeth sought solace on the balcony, hoping to catch a breath of fresh air. However, her plans were interrupted by the approach of a gentleman dressed in a red coat. They had not yet been formally introduced.

"Excuse me. I know this is all untoward, but I could not help but overhear you speaking just now to your friend Miss Lucas about Pemberley in Derbyshire."

Elizabeth's heart slammed against her chest. Standing before her was a gentleman who was the epitome of beauty—a fine countenance, an Adonis-like figure, and a very pleasing address. His handsome features alone were sufficient to forgive his breach of propriety, enticing Elizabeth to seize the opportunity to become better acquainted with him. Adorned in military attire, he was undoubtedly a member of the militia stationed near Meryton.

Caution should have prevailed, yet Elizabeth's eagerness to discuss Pemberley overcame her better judgment. *Surely, this gentleman must be familiar with the Darcys.*

"I beg your pardon, sir," Elizabeth replied coolly, feigning less interest in the stranger than she truly possessed.

"Allow me to introduce myself. I am Lieutenant George Wickham, at your service," he said, bowing gallantly. Rising to his full height, he continued, "And may I ask your name?"

"I am afraid it would be improper to introduce myself to a complete stranger, sir."

"Indeed, you are correct. However, how can we overcome this inconvenience unless you reveal your name to me?"

"A conundrum indeed," Elizabeth teased.

The gentleman cast a brief glance in the direction of the doorway. "No doubt you are acquainted with many of the evening's gathering. Perhaps a mutual acquaintance could assist me as I am determined to discover your name."

"Well, sir, as this is my uncle and aunt's residence, I trust that, being a fellow guest, you are aware of the necessary protocol."

With those words, Elizabeth curtsied and departed, hopeful that the handsome stranger would take the initiative and secure a proper introduction.

She made her way to where her friend Charlotte stood engaging in conversation with her younger sister Mariah. Shortly thereafter, Elizabeth's uncle Mr. Phillips caught her attention, crossing the room to join her with the captivating stranger, still lingering in her thoughts, now positioned beside her uncle.

"Lizzy, my dear, this fine young officer has informed me of his desire to make your acquaintance, and he has enlisted my help in introducing himself to you." Uncle Phillips stepped aside, allowing the man to stand directly before Elizabeth.

"May I present Lieutenant George Wickham? Lieutenant Wickham, this is my lovely niece, Miss Bennet."

Elizabeth accepted the introduction in the customary manner, disregarding the gentleman's earlier breach of decorum. After exchanging a few words with her and with Lieutenant Wickham, her uncle excused himself, leaving Elizabeth alone with the officer.

George Wickham immediately began recounting his experiences at Pemberley, sharing details of his upbringing and how Lady Anne Darcy had forced him to leave when he was thirteen.

"Lady Anne? I do not understand. Why would her ladyship send you away from Pemberley?" Elizabeth asked, perplexed. This portrayal of the esteemed lady contradicted everything she knew about the woman who had taken her in as a child, raising her as her own daughter.

"The reason is quite simple," Mr. Wickham explained. "She despised me. Not only did she consider me a threat to her son, Fitzwilliam Darcy, but she also harbored jealousy toward me."

"Jealousy? Why would Lady Anne Darcy be jealous of you?" Elizabeth asked. This depiction of the great lady did not align with her understanding of the woman who had shown her such love and care.

"I believe it had much to do with her husband's high opinion of me. Mr. Darcy intended to be my godfather, at least initially. However, once Lady Anne learned of his intentions, a long-lost grandfather whom I had never known arrived at Pemberley and took me away from the only home I had ever known. Mr. Darcy was powerless to stop him due to our familial ties. Given the chance, I would have undoubtedly remained at Pemberley. Alas, even my own father, Mr. Darcy's steward at the time, did not oppose my being taken away."

"I am sorry to hear that you were unable to stay in the only home you had ever known during the early years of your life. But how can Lady Anne be held accountable if your grandfather came to get you? Surely he must have done so of his own volition and with your best interest at heart."

The gentleman scoffed. "I am certain my grandfather would not have come if Lady Anne had not gone to extraordinary lengths to find him."

"Why do you think she would go to such extremes?"

"As I mentioned, she despised me. She believed I would have a negative influence on her precious son, the future master of Pemberley. She was determined to remove me from his life by any means necessary. When Mr. Darcy expressed his desire to be my godfather, it only fueled her resolve to remove me from her home and, ultimately, her life."

"And what of your relationship with Mr. Darcy himself or even with Fitzwilliam?" Elizabeth cautiously inquired, mindful not to appear too curious.

"Fitzwilliam?" Wickham repeated, arching his brow. "Are you and he so intimately acquainted that you address him by his given name? I cannot recall anyone outside his immediate circle referring to him in such a manner."

Elizabeth felt a warmth creeping into her cheeks. She had not intended to disclose her close connection to the Darcys, especially their son. First, she needed to ascertain the stranger's true intentions. If his claims held any truth, did he not have valid reasons to harbor ill feelings toward Lady Anne?

"While it is true that I share a history with the Darcys, I dare not discuss it now. Such a conversation would require more time than we have this evening."

"I shall not press the matter. Perhaps, with time, you will feel comfortable sharing with me as openly as I have with you. As for my relationship with Mr. Darcy and his son, I would say it is practically nonexistent. I did maintain correspondence with the elder Mr. Darcy for a time, but eventually, all communication ceased."

"And his son?" Elizabeth asked.

"He was away at Matlock when my grandfather came to take me from Pemberley. We have had no contact since we were young boys." Wickham shrugged. "But I am not surprised. While Mr. Darcy is the finest man I know, his son takes after his mother—haughty, proud, and raised to look down upon those deemed beneath him in society. He is nothing to me. Were we to meet, I am sure we would be no more than indifferent acquaintances," said Wickham, brushing invisible lint from his sleeve.

Suddenly just standing there conversing with this man caused Elizabeth a bit of discomfort. She was unwavering in her loyalty to the Darcys. The last thing she wished to do was engage in a debate about the family's character with a stranger, even if his words struck a chord within her regarding Lady Anne prompting the resurfacing of her own lingering concerns. Elizabeth was confident that any distress Lady Anne may have experienced due to her departure from Pemberley was alleviated by the distance that now separated Fitzwilliam and herself.

For that reason alone, she had to give some credence to Lieutenant Wickham's account. If Lady Anne truly deemed him unsuitable for her son's company, even as a young boy, why would she not employ every means at her disposal to remove him from Pemberley?

As the devoted mother she is, whose foremost priority is to shield her son from undesirable influences, why would she not exert all her power in order to have her way?

Chapter 18 - Exasperation

Elizabeth's equanimity had been sorely tested by days of avoiding Longbourn's exasperating houseguest. Seeking solace, she stole away and stationed herself by the tranquil pond, finding respite in the serene beauty of its still waters. However, her momentary peace shattered when she glimpsed him approaching, steadily making his way towards her. A surge of desperation coursed through her, yearning for a means of escape that would spare her from his company. Were there such a means short of diving into the water, she surely would have taken it, but alas, no such exit existed, and she resigned herself to the inevitable encounter.

Soon enough, Elizabeth found herself standing nervously in front of Mr. Collins, uncertainty swirling within her. In the brief span of their acquaintance, she had developed an intense aversion to her distant cousin, harboring profound disdain for his pompous and self-important demeanor.

"Cousin Elizabeth," Mr. Collins began, his voice tinged with an odd mixture of formality and forced enthusiasm, "I have sought you out today with a specific purpose in mind—to make a proposal of marriage to you."

Elizabeth felt her heart sink. The dreaded moment of truth with Mr. Collins was upon her. She knew her father would expect her to be courteous, so she took a deep breath and composed herself.

He cleared his throat nervously, adjusting his collar with exaggerated precision. "As your estimable cousin and a clergyman, I believe it is my duty to seek a suitable match, and in my discernment, I have concluded that you possess the qualities I seek in a wife. Your beauty, intelligence, and deference to familial obligation make you an ideal candidate to grace the esteemed position of being Mrs. Collins."

A mixture of disbelief and incredulity swirled within Elizabeth. His words, while intended as a compliment, were hollow and devoid of any genuine sentiment. It was clear to her that Mr. Collins was driven more by societal expectations and the pursuit of a convenient match rather than a sincere connection.

With measured poise, Elizabeth said, "Mr. Collins, I appreciate the honor you bestow upon me with your proposal. However, I must respectfully decline."

The gentleman looked taken aback. "Decline? But Cousin Elizabeth, I assure you, I would make a most excellent husband. I have a comfortable living as vicar of Hunsford, and my connections are impeccable, as are your own, having lived with the Darcys of Pemberley in Derbyshire for most of your life. Think of the advantages. Our alliance will be most advantageous and would be a source of great happiness for so many of our acquaintances."

"I am more concerned for my happiness and, ironically, yours too. In the short time I have known you, I have never been more convinced of the lack of suitability among two people. A marriage between the two of us would no doubt subject both of us to misery of the acutest kind."

"Have you no other reasons for your injudicious reply other than your belief that we would not be happy? I assure you that happiness in marriage is not simply a matter of chance. It is also a matter of choice."

Elizabeth hesitated for a moment before replying, the memory of her time in Derbyshire with Fitzwilliam weighing heavily on her heart. "I have other reasons, Mr. Collins. I cannot marry someone whom I do not love, nor can I enter into a marriage based solely on the advantages it may bring to others."

Mr. Collins frowned. "Love? What does love have to do with it? Marriage is a practical matter, and you would do well to remember that. Besides, I am offering you security and a comfortable living—a chance to live here at Longbourn when your father passes. You know very well that is his favorite wish for you. What more could you want?"

Elizabeth's eyes flashed with anger. "I want happiness, Mr. Collins. I want to marry someone who respects me as an equal, who values my opinions and interests, and who can make me laugh even in the darkest of times. You, sir, are not that person."

Mr. Collins looked crestfallen, but Elizabeth felt no sympathy for him. She had no intention of sacrificing her happiness for the sake of propriety and social expectations.

"I must insist that you reconsider, Cousin Elizabeth," Mr. Collins said, his voice strained. "I am offering you an excellent match, and it would be a shame to let girlish notions cloud your judgment."

Elizabeth shook her head. "It is not so-called girlish notions that guide my decision, Mr. Collins, but rather a desire for genuine love and affection in a marriage. I thank you for your offer, but I cannot accept it."

Mr. Collins bristled with indignation. "You will come to regret this decision, Cousin Elizabeth. I am a highly respectable and well-connected gentleman, and you will find no better offer than mine in the future."

Elizabeth remained steadfast in her conviction. "I will not regret it, Mr. Collins. I am content to wait for someone who loves me and whom I love in return."

Mr. Collins sneered at her. "You are a foolish girl—foolish and imprudent. You have been spoiled by living at Pemberley, surrounded by wealth and luxury. You have forgotten your place in society, and it will be a rude awakening for you when you realize that you will never find a better match than me."

Elizabeth's fiery temper ignited. Her voice edged with defiance, she said, "I am well aware of my place in society, Mr. Collins." Her eyes blazing with unwavering resolve, she continued, "I refuse to be forced into a marriage that would be unhappy and unfulfilling. I would rather remain unmarried for the rest of my life than enter such a union."

A flicker of frustration danced across Mr. Collins' face, quickly masked by a feigned air of indifference. "Very well, Cousin," he huffed, his tone laden with a mix of resignation and arrogance. "I see that there is no swaying your stubborn heart. But mark my words, you will rue this decision. Good day."

Watching him as he stormed away, a tumultuous blend of relief and apprehension coursed through her. She knew deep within her heart that she had made the right choice in rejecting her ridiculous cousin, yet the lingering realization weighed upon her that this likely would not be the last instance she would need to defend her decision to remain unwed. Memories of a rejected suitor during her coming out season flooded her mind, vividly etched in her thoughts like an indelible mark. She was transported back to that encounter, reliving the scene with intense clarity.

In her recollection, the suitor emerged, his refined manners and impeccable lineage rendering him the epitome of an ideal match in the eyes of society. However, Elizabeth had detected emptiness behind his polished facade, a lack of genuine connection that left her unimpressed and decidedly against him.

Reminding herself of her present predicament, Elizabeth silently considered, *I am determined to stay true to myself, no matter what the future holds.*

Suffering the discomfort of the unpleasant exchange with Mr. Collins, Elizabeth made her way to her father's study. Her heart was pounding, her chest heaving with the pent-up frustration of their conversation. The scent of leather-bound books and worn parchment greeted her as she entered, bringing a sense of familiarity and nostalgia.

Mr. Bennet was settled behind his imposing mahogany desk, engrossed in a book. Looking up at her entrance, he flashed a knowing grin. "So, Lizzy, my dear, should I be wishing you joy?" he asked, mischief twinkling in his eyes.

Elizabeth raised her eyebrows. *So this is how it is.*

Crossing her arms over her chest, she stared her father down. "Perhaps it is I who should be offering congratulations, Papa," she retorted, her voice dripping with a quiet fury she scarcely managed to hold in check. "Is this not what you wanted? To have Mr. Collins as a son-in-law?"

The unexpected turn of her words seemed to propel Mr. Bennet to his feet. His chair scraped backward, the sound echoing through the hushed room. "If you supposed for one instance that, having met Mr. Collins, I would willingly accept an alliance between you two, then you really do not know me at all." He sighed, wiping a weary hand over his face. "Not that I blame you. I owe it all to myself."

Elizabeth's expression softened a touch. "Then why, Papa," she asked, "did you allow me to suffer the man's company out of fear of disappointing you?"

A long silence was filled only by the clock ticking on the mantle. Mr. Bennet's gaze was fixed on his daughter, his eyes reflecting a deep regret. It was then that Elizabeth knew she had struck a chord, hitting a nerve with her pointed question.

Eventually, she sighed, feeling a strange mix of sadness and relief. "I did not accept his proposal, Papa," she admitted. "Mr. Collins is the last man in the world I could be prevailed upon to marry."

The relief that washed over Mr. Bennet's face was palpable, a physical embodiment of the breath he had been holding since her arrival in the study. "Oh, Lizzy," he murmured, flopping back in his chair. "Thank heavens for that."

However, the knowing twinkle was back in his eyes as he leaned forward, his hands steepled in front of him. "But mind you, my dear," he added, his voice heavy with paternal affection and a hint of warning, "having rejected Mr. Collins, you are now free to suffer heartbreak and disappointed hopes of your own. And lest you should forget, our world can be especially unkind to those who choose to follow their hearts."

Elizabeth could only nod, her mind already

swirling with thoughts of what was to come. But for now, she felt a sense of peace in knowing her father understood her decision, even if he could not entirely sympathize with the choices she might make in the future. The path she was forging for herself was her own to walk, no matter how uncertain it seemed.

Chapter 19 - Consideration

Charlotte Lucas walked down the dirt path toward her home, her thoughts on Mr. Collins. While he was not the most attractive or interesting of men, he was a respectable man with a good position as a clergyman. Charlotte knew she was not getting any younger and needed to secure her future. Mr. Collins' proposal seemed like a good opportunity. She had always thought marriage was simply a means to an end—a way to secure her future and a comfortable life. But now that she had been offered a proposal, she began to question her own beliefs. Was it really enough to marry for convenience, especially if it might cost her a most cherished friendship?

Despite the short duration of their acquaintance, Elizabeth was already one of her closest friends. She had quickly taken to Elizabeth's wit and intelligence and felt a kinship with the woman that had been absent in her life for so long. It was a relief to talk openly and share her thoughts and feelings without fear of judgment or ridicule.

The next day was a day like any other, and Charlotte had come to call on Elizabeth to catch up with her and share some news.

"Elizabeth," Charlotte began as soon as she was seated, "I have some news I would like to share with you."

Elizabeth smiled. "I am always interested to hear any news. What has happened?"

Charlotte sighed heavily and bit her lip before speaking. "Mr. Collins has proposed to me."

Elizabeth's eyes widened in surprise. "Mr. Collins?"

Charlotte nodded. "Yes, Mr. Collins has proposed marriage to me." She paused, fidgeting with her hands. "I wanted to come and tell you because I wanted you to know that I do not wish to accept his offer unless I have your approval. You see, I want you to know that I would not take a place that rightly belongs to you."

Elizabeth smiled, touched by her friend's concern. "Charlotte, you must do whatever is best for you and your future. I do not wish you to deny Mr. Collins' proposal simply out of concern for me. I hardly know him, nor do I have any designs on him. You must make the decision that is best for you and your future."

Charlotte breathed a sigh of contentment, for her friend's response had brought her the assurance she had so dearly sought; that Elizabeth should not be aggrieved upon learning that an opportunity which was meant to be hers, had been offered instead to Charlotte.

"Thank you, Elizabeth," Charlotte said. "Your words mean a great deal to me. I shall take your advice and make my decision based on what I feel is best for me."

The two women shared a few more pleasantries before Charlotte made her way home. She felt a sense of peace now that her mind was made up. She could accept Mr. Collins' proposal and not feel guilty for taking something that did not belong to her. Elizabeth had given her blessing, and that was enough.

After bidding farewell to Charlotte, Elizabeth retreated to the solitude of her favorite reading nook. Here, amid the rows of well-loved books, she began to unravel her feelings concerning the unexpected revelation from her friend.

Mr. Collins, the awkward and obsequious man, had proposed to Charlotte, one of her most cherished friends. It was a development that left her feelings muddled and emotions stirred, having spent a good deal of time with Mr. Collins recently and finding him insufferable. His self-importance, pompousness, and sycophantic deference to Lady Catherine were unbearable. The prospect of sharing a life with him would have been nothing short of a disaster for her, a fiery personality who thrived on intellectual discourse and independence.

However, other thoughts began to permeate Elizabeth's mind as she settled back against the plush, cushioned armchair. Having engaged in numerous conversations with her friend about matters of love and marriage, Elizabeth was acutely aware of Charlotte's circumstances. She understood how Charlotte herself grappled with the notion of becoming a burden to her family due to her advancing age and lack of prospects.

Perhaps the clergyman's insipidity would be tolerable, even beneficial for Charlotte, with her practical and composed demeanor. Maybe her friend's pragmatic approach to marriage as a means to an end, more than a union of affection, would enable her to lead a comfortable life with Mr. Collins. Elizabeth was not blind to the realities of their world, a world in which women were often constrained by their marital choices, where wealth and security were prized over love and compatibility.

My own experience with the Darcys is proof enough of that, is it not?

Still, Elizabeth's heart ached for Charlotte, for the sacrifice she was prepared to make. But there was a sliver of relief that bubbled within her. Charlotte's acceptance of Mr. Collins' proposal would mean he would soon leave Longbourn, providing Elizabeth with the sweet solace of his absence. A quiet, soothing peace settled in her heart as she allowed herself to indulge in this thought.

I daresay this arrangement will lead to a comfortable life for Charlotte and simultaneously free Longbourn from the constant vexation of Mr. Collins' company.

Chapter 20 - Confrontation

Lady Catherine de Bourgh, a woman of unwavering determination and commanding presence, strode about the quaint garden at Longbourn with an air of purpose. Her towering figure and stern countenance demanded attention, and she never failed to carry her point. On this particular day, a singular mission fueled her arrival—to extract answers from the audacious young woman who had dared to reject her vicar's proposal.

As Elizabeth approached, her eyes met Lady Catherine's penetrating glare. The very atmosphere seemed to quiver under the magnitude of their impending confrontation. Upon standing face-to-face, the haughty lady wasted no time, her words laden with undisguised contempt.

"Miss Bennet, I have come here to speak with you about a most disturbing matter that was recently brought to my attention," she said, her voice dripping with contempt. What better evidence could there be of her ladyship's newly cemented low opinion of her sister's former ward than her use of Elizabeth's formal appellation?

A flicker of amusement danced in Elizabeth's eyes, hidden beneath her composed facade. She knew all too well the effect her defiance had on Lady Catherine, and she relished the opportunity to further test the officious aristocrat's patience. Calmly, she raised an elegant eyebrow. "And what, pray tell, do you wish to discuss, Lady Catherine?" Elizabeth asked, with a hint of sardonic curiosity in her tone.

The tension in the air grew palpable as these two formidable women prepared themselves for a battle of wills. They stood in the picturesque gardens of Longbourn, surrounded by vibrant blooms that whispered their secrets to the gentle breeze. The late afternoon sunlight cascaded through the branches of ancient trees, casting intricate patterns of light and shadow on the ground. It was a scene of serene beauty that stood in stark contrast to the storm brewing between Lady Catherine and Elizabeth.

Her ladyship, undeterred by the picturesque surroundings, regarded Elizabeth with a mixture of disdain and determination. Her voice, sharp as a blade, sliced through the tranquility. "Your behavior toward Mr. Collins, my vicar, has been nothing short of abominable. I demand an explanation for your audacity."

Elizabeth's lips curled into a knowing smile as she tilted her head, her eyes sparkling with an irrepressible spirit. With measured grace, she met Lady Catherine's icy stare, her voice carrying an undercurrent of suppressed defiance. "Lady Catherine, I believe I have conducted myself with the utmost propriety."

"Propriety? I daresay you do not comprehend the meaning of the word. Propriety dictates you do what is in the best interest of you and your family. Why on earth did you reject Mr. Collins' marriage proposal?" Lady Catherine asked, her eyes narrowing. "He is an honorable and decent man, and you can by no means expect a better offer than the one he made."

Elizabeth sighed. "I am afraid I cannot accept your assessment of Mr. Collins, Lady Catherine," she said calmly. "While he may be respectable, he is not the right match for me."

"You cannot be guaranteed to receive such a similarly advantageous proposal of marriage, despite your having been reared at Pemberley by my sister and her husband."

"If what you say is true and I am forced to live my life in spinsterhood, what can that matter to you?"

Lady Catherine frowned. "You are being foolish, young woman," she said. "And I suspect it has something to do with your feelings for my nephew, Fitzwilliam."

Elizabeth felt her face flush with anger. "I hardly see how that is your concern, Lady Catherine," she said coolly.

"It is my concern," her ladyship said, her voice rising. "I know all about your role in turning my nephew against my daughter, Anne. How many times have you heard my family speak of my nephew's engagement to my Anne? While it is true that the engagement between them is of a peculiar kind, that does not make it less binding. From their infancy, they have been intended for each other. It is the favorite wish of his mother, as well as of hers. While in their cradles, we planned the union. Yet you, young woman, persist in thwarting our aspirations as though you are lost to every feeling of propriety and delicacy.

"I thought that by throwing Mr. Collins in your path, I could solve the problem. Even your own father was privy to the scheme, hence his insistence that you return to Hertfordshire as a means of reversing the adverse impact of the entail on his estate once he is gone. But it seems you are still holding out on the possibility of an alliance with Fitzwilliam."

Elizabeth's anger turned to confusion. *Surely her ladyship's mention of my father is meant to besmirch our relationship.* "I am not sure what you are getting at, Lady Catherine," she said, feeling a knot form in her stomach.

"Do not pretend to be ignorant," Lady Catherine said sharply. "You have been nursing a tender regard for my nephew for years. And look at where it has landed you. It has been months since you left Derbyshire, and yet my nephew has made no effort to see you, which speaks volumes about his feelings for you or lack thereof. Whereas he has spent a prodigious amount of time with my Anne. Now, what have you to say about that?"

Elizabeth felt her heart sink as Lady Catherine's words hit her like a cascade of falling rocks. It was true that she had long harbored feelings for Fitzwilliam Darcy but had tried to bury them deep within her heart. However, hearing Lady Catherine's accusation made her realize that perhaps she had not been as successful in hiding them as she had thought.

"I have nothing to say on the matter, Lady Catherine," Elizabeth said. "My feelings for Fitzwilliam are my concern and have nothing to do with your nephew's actions or lack thereof. You are wasting your time as well as my own, and I must insist you concern yourself with your own family affairs and leave mine alone."

"The possibility of you ruining the favorite wish of our family by standing in the way of the union between Anne and Fitzwilliam is a matter of grave concern for both our families."

"How can it be? You said Fitzwilliam has not tried to seek me out, insinuating that spending time with your daughter is his preference."

"Do you doubt it?"

"I highly suspect you are the one with doubts; otherwise, you would not have traveled all this way."

Lady Catherine hesitated for a moment, and

then said, "I came to make it clear to you that I will not abide any interference from you. My nephew has not sought you out, but that is not to say your paths will never cross in the future. Should that happen, you are to do everything in your power to discourage any romantic inclinations he may harbor toward you."

Elizabeth could feel the anger bubbling up inside her. Her courage always rose with any attempt to intimidate her. "I will not be told how to act by you, Lady Catherine," she said, her voice rising. "And I certainly will not allow anyone to dictate my feelings or actions toward any man, including your nephew."

Her ladyship narrowed her eyes. "I know you credit yourself for your impertinence, but I will not countenance it, especially not in this matter. I demand your promise to relinquish any foolish notion you may harbor regarding a future with my nephew!"

The audacity of this woman to come all this way and behave so officiously is beyond the pale.

Elizabeth could feel her temperature rising, an internal fire stoked by the presence of the uninvited guest. "I cannot make such a promise to anyone, especially not to someone so wholly unconnected to me as you are, Lady Catherine," she said firmly.

The haughty woman's countenance turned icy. "And what of my sister, Lady Anne?" she asked. "Surely you owe her some obligation for all she did for you. Accepting you into her home when even your own father wanted nothing to do with you. Is this your gratitude for her attentions to you this past decade?"

Elizabeth felt her heart sink at the mention of Lady Anne. She had always felt a deep sense of gratefulness toward the woman who had taken her in as a child and raised her as her own.

"Whatever my obligations may be to Lady Anne, they are none of your concern, Lady Catherine," Elizabeth said, her voice laced with steel. "You can rest assured that I will always do what is in my best interest, with no consideration for your desires."

Lady Catherine's eyes widened with disbelief. "How dare you speak to me in such a manner, young woman!" she exclaimed. "You forget to whom you are speaking."

"I am speaking to a woman who has no right to demand anything of me," Elizabeth said. "I owe you nothing, Lady Catherine. And I will not be bullied into submission by your threats."

For a moment, Lady Catherine was silent as she glared at Elizabeth. But then, with a sneer, she turned on her heel and began to make her way toward the gate.

"We are not done here," she said over her shoulder. "And you had better prepare yourself for the wrath of both Fitzwilliam women. You will learn once and for all that the Fitzwilliam sisters are not to be trifled with."

And with that, she was gone, leaving Elizabeth with mixed emotions—anger, confusion, and a sense of foreboding. Elizabeth stood there for a few moments, trying to regain her composure. How ironic that the last thing Elizabeth ever wanted to do was sacrifice her own desire in favor of Lady Catherine's dictates. So long as Lady Anne was against any possible alliance between Elizabeth and Fitzwilliam, Elizabeth was duty-bound not to oppose her.

Chapter 21 - Aspiration

ALL OF MERYTON and the surrounding villages were excited about the news of Netherfield Park, for it was reported that a single man of a large fortune from the north had purchased it. After so many years of neglect, Netherfield Park was to be occupied at last. At least, that was the hope of so many. This prospect excited those from every walk of life, for it meant new employment for tradespeople and laborers and possibly a future son-in-law for the eager mammas with unwed daughters to get rid of. Who did not know that where there was one single young man with a fortune, there were most likely two? What a delightful prospect indeed.

Even Elizabeth could confess to being a little

excited upon first hearing such speculations. She was at the neighboring village of Lucas Lodge, visiting with her friend Charlotte when she first heard the news.

"I declare this is a happy prospect for the single young ladies in our neighborhood," cried Lady Lucas, Charlotte's mother whose business in life was gossiping and marrying off her two daughters. "Dare I hope what with Charlotte's advantageous engagement to Mr. Collins, my Mariah might very well be the next mistress of Netherfield?"

Elizabeth and Charlotte threw each other a look that went unnoticed by the proud mamma.

"I was just telling your father that he ought to be the first to go to Netherfield Park and greet the newcomer," she said to Charlotte. "Indeed, there is no better candidate than your father for the job, what with his being the highest-ranking member of our society. Your father is as good as a peer, is he not?"

As was her custom in these instances, Charlotte merely acquiesced with a slight nod. Elizabeth could not help but laugh inside at the prospect of having such a mother whose primary aim was getting rid of her daughters. It occurred to her that it was not just the nobles who spent their time conspiring to make matches for their children. Lady Anne's constant reminding Elizabeth that she too would be prevailed on to take a husband and how it was Lady Anne's responsibility to see that she made the best match possible came to mind.

So long as it is not a match with her only son and Pemberley's heir, Elizabeth inwardly mused. No matter how hard she tried, she found it impossible to banish thoughts of Fitzwilliam from her mind. She was always contemplating his possible whereabouts and pursuits, the physical separation not diminishing her affection. Elizabeth acknowledged that her feelings for Fitzwilliam Darcy would always hold a special place in her heart, regardless of their respective future marital alliances.

As the conversation flowed, a startling possibility dawned upon Elizabeth. The gentleman in question, the new master of Netherfield, could it possibly be Fitzwilliam? Elizabeth knew that property acquisition was not an unfamiliar endeavor for the Darcy family, as they owned vast expanses across England. However, the prospect of Fitzwilliam purchasing this particular estate in this particular region caused her to ponder. She could not help but wonder: if Fitzwilliam had indeed bought the estate abutting Longbourn Village, could he have possibly done it for her?

An unexpected wave of emotions crashed over Elizabeth as she endeavored to discern the validity of her burgeoning suspicion. With a bemused expression, Elizabeth turned toward Lady Lucas and, with a voice concealing her inner turmoil, asked, "Pray, do we know anything more about this mysterious gentleman, apart from his considerable fortune and unmarried status?"

Lady Lucas, relishing the opportunity to share her bounty of gossip, replied with an air of importance, "Not a great deal, my dear. The estate agent was most secretive. However, he let slip that the gentleman is from the north, possesses a noble bearing, and has a fondness for well-managed estates."

The north. The very same direction as Derbyshire. Elizabeth felt her heartbeat quicken. And his fondness for well-managed estates could certainly apply to Fitzwilliam, a man of impeccable taste and a deep-rooted sense of responsibility toward his family's extensive properties. The pieces of the puzzle seemed to fall into place, yet Elizabeth was cautious not to let her imagination run wild.

Having been a silent observer till now, Charlotte said, "Well, if the gentleman is as genteel and prosperous as reported, he certainly will be a welcome addition to our society, will he not?"

Elizabeth smiled. "Indeed, he will be. I believe we are all rather eager to meet the enigmatic proprietor."

She left the conversation at that, but inwardly, Elizabeth's busy mind was eagerly engaged. The likelihood of Fitzwilliam being the new owner of Netherfield was too significant to disregard. She pondered the prospect and the potential implications, her heart fluttering with anticipation, trepidation, and a healthy dosage of hope.

The man who had unintentionally captivated her heart, could he truly be near? Elizabeth determined that time would reveal the truth of the matter. Until then, she would engage in the happenings of her daily life as usual, with the thought of Fitzwilliam and all that being reunited with him could entail fueling her spirits and secretly enlivening her heart.

Chapter 22 - Anticipation

THE FIRST PLACE that Fitzwilliam Darcy visited after his arrival at his recently acquired estate was Longbourn Village. Why would he not, given his connection with the Bennets? No one could question his motives, even if he knew there was only one purpose behind his actions. He desperately missed Elizabeth and longed to see her again. They had been apart for long enough.

However, upon his arrival at Longbourn that morning, Elizabeth was not there. She was away from home, making morning calls. Thus, Fitzwilliam and Mr. Bennet sat alone in the drawing room, facing each other.

"I understand you are the new owner of

Netherfield Park, young man," Mr. Bennet remarked.

Fitzwilliam nodded.

"Congratulations," said Bennet. "It is indeed a fine property, although it badly needs repair."

Fitzwilliam nodded once again. He knew Mr. Bennet to be a sardonic man who took pride in his mocking wit. Until he knew what the man sitting opposite him was about, he decided to keep his cards close to his chest.

"I imagine there are thousands of such properties spread throughout England. Why did you settle on Netherfield Park, if you do not mind my asking? I hope your reasoning has nothing to do with its proximity to my humble abode."

"Actually, Mr. Bennet, my decision to choose Netherfield Park has everything to do with its proximity to your home. I hope you did not persuade yourself that I would wish to be far away from Elizabeth forever."

"Elizabeth?" the older man repeated, raising an eyebrow.

"Would you have me refer to one of my dearest acquaintances in some other way?"

"For the sake of propriety, I believe you should

… nay, you must, else our friends and neighbors might start suspecting a stronger connection between the two of you than what we know to be true."

The parlor door swung open just then, and Elizabeth entered with a bright smile. She hurried to the guest's side. "Fitzwilliam!" The two young people embraced, but not too long before Elizabeth remembered herself. She blushed and stepped back, curtsying.

Following her lead, Fitzwilliam bowed. "It is a pleasure to see you."

"The pleasure is all mine," Elizabeth said. "You are looking very well."

He simply smiled in response.

"Please, have a seat." She turned to her father. "Have you called for tea?"

"No, I am afraid I have been engrossed in conversation with our guest," Mr. Bennet replied.

Elizabeth took up the task of doing what her father should have done. She always knew her father held severe reservations over where he felt Fitzwilliam's motives tended, but that was no excuse for incivility.

"I, too, am looking forward to 'being

engrossed' in conversation with you, sir," she said teasingly to her guest.

"Perhaps we can go horse riding when we are done here," said Fitzwilliam. "I know how much you love doing that."

"I do not know that I can spare the horse," said Mr. Bennet. "That is unless you came equipped with a spare horse of your own."

"Actually, sir, I did." He looked at Elizabeth. "I brought Bella with me."

"How wonderful!" Elizabeth exclaimed with energy. "I have missed riding her very much."

"How thoughtful of you," said Mr. Bennet.

"Is Bella here or perhaps at Netherfield?" Elizabeth asked. "I understand you are the estate's new owner."

"Indeed. When I learned Netherfield Park was available for sale, I seized the chance to become its new owner. I have such plans for the estate. Given its current state, I am sure I will be quite busy with all its renovations."

"It is not as though Netherfield has not been available for years," Bennet said.

Ignoring her father's retort, Elizabeth said, "I have never actually gone into the house, but given its closeness to Longbourn Village, I dare confess to having walked about the park with impunity. As its new owner, I trust you will forgive my trespasses."

"As the new owner, I hope you will avail yourself of the chance to walk about the park as often as you like. In fact, I am depending upon it."

When the servant entered the room to lay out the tea things for Elizabeth, Mr. Bennet arose from his chair.

"If the two of you will pardon me, I believe I shall seek shelter in the solace of my study. As much as I have enjoyed this little reunion, the book I was reading calls out to me." He folded his paper and tucked it under his arm. "Mr. Darcy," he said, bowing slightly. And then he was gone, leaving Fitzwilliam and Elizabeth alone in the room.

Moments later, Elizabeth's companion entered the room and pleasantly greeted the guest, given her connection to his family back in Derbyshire. She then took a chair near the window. Apparently, she meant to supervise the young couple, and given the timing of her appearance, no doubt at Mr. Bennet's instruction.

It was just as well, for by now, Elizabeth had gotten past the excitement of being reunited with the one man in the world who had ever held her heart, and she started to recall the reason they had been separated in the first place or at least part of the reason.

She could not regret coming to Longbourn to live with her father, for he needed her, and she needed him too. But she would forever feel the nagging disappointment that Lady Anne, whom Elizabeth loved as much as if she were her own mother, did not deem her a suitable prospect as a future daughter-in-law.

With Lady Anne hundreds of miles away and Fitzwilliam sitting there directly beside her, how would Elizabeth keep her tacit promise to the former and her distance from the latter? She always loved spending time with Fitzwilliam. She missed him more than she ever thought possible, and now they were together again.

I will not think of any of that today. Perhaps I will not think of any of that tomorrow, either. I have wished for this day for too long not to enjoy every single minute of it.

With that thought in mind, Elizabeth said, "So, when shall we begin our ride? It is far too lovely a day to remain indoors. I know exactly the place we should go. But first, I shall have Cook prepare a basket for who is to say how long we will be."

"I am at your service, young lady," said Fitzwilliam. Then, changing the subject, he said, "I see your father seems to suffer some reservations where I am concerned."

"I hope you do not take it personally, Fitzwilliam. Are fathers not well within their rights to be protective where their daughters are concerned?" Elizabeth asked. All the while, she could only think of Fitzwilliam's own parents. Were they not just as protective where their son was concerned?

Part of her wondered if she should confide in Fitzwilliam, his mother's reservations toward her. She did not mean to be the means of alienating the mother from the son. She cared about both of them too much to do anything of the sort.

If only my feelings for Lady Anne's son could be likened to a younger sister's feelings toward an older brother. Certainly, that would have made her ladyship happy, but it was not to be.

Elizabeth could not control her heart's love for the man sitting beside her, just as she could not stop the sun from rising in the east or the stars from shining at night.

There was a time, however, when Elizabeth feared the affection Fitzwilliam obviously felt toward her was, in her mind, akin to brotherly love. He had always promised to protect her and to remain by her side, forever her faithful servant and the one to do her bidding.

Were those just as likely to be the sentiments of an overly protective older sibling as the words of a lover? But each occasion that brought him back home to Pemberley taught her to think differently. Instead of growing further apart, as time and distance must surely dictate for a young man who was coming of age, they became increasingly inseparable, rarely making time for others. And when they were forced to be apart, they counted the days until they would be together again.

"Of course, your father has every right," Fitzwilliam replied, bringing Elizabeth back to the present. "But why must he be wary of me? He should know that I mean you no harm. He ought to know that I am your most devoted protector. No one is more important to me than you are."

"Well, perhaps that is the problem. Maybe my

father fears that your true motive in being here is to persuade me to return with you to Derbyshire."

"Of course, I am happiest when we are in Derbyshire together, but I know how important it is for you to be here with your father. I would never dare take this opportunity away from you. I would never wish to be the means of keeping the two of you apart."

"Hence your purchasing Netherfield Park... You mean to be here to watch over me. Or do I presume too much?"

"You know me too well not to know why I have come, Elizabeth."

"As happy as I am to have you so near, how shall we proceed? Are we to feign indifference toward each other so as not to excite the curiosity of others or are we to proceed as we did while in Derbyshire, in which case we must surely disappoint all the eager mammas in want of a wealthy husband for their single daughters."

"I am happy to do as you wish, Elizabeth. I have only one true purpose in being here."

"I think we should exercise caution, Fitzwilliam."

"If that is your wish," he said.

"I ... I believe it would be better for everyone concerned."

"Does that mean we must give up our early morning walks in the countryside?"

She shook her head. "I would not say that. I mean to say I do love to walk, and it is not as though I can dictate the morning rituals of others."

"And what about horse riding?"

"Well, someone has to ride Bella. It might as well be me. By the way, should she be stabled at Longbourn or Netherfield?"

"I am unsure if it would be wise to keep her at Longbourn."

"Why not? Are you concerned that the stable at Longbourn is not suitable for Bella?"

"Well, she is a thoroughbred mare, descended from prize-winning horses on both sides. She might attract some unwanted attention, to say the least."

"Are you worried she might be stolen?" Elizabeth paused for a moment. "Or perhaps you fear that my father might gamble her away."

"I never said that."

"Then what are you saying?"

"Do you not think others would misconstrue my bringing you such a prized possession?"

"I suppose you have a point. So, Netherfield it is," Elizabeth concluded.

After some time, Fitzwilliam spoke up again. "You mentioned the possibility of your father gambling the horse away. Has he had a relapse?"

"I wish I could say he is fully recovered since we returned, but that would be wishful thinking on my part."

"I am sorry to hear that. I cannot bear to think of you suffering because of it."

"Oh, no! It is not as bad as all that, at least not that I know. It is just that my father appears to have starts and stops when it comes to such things. I know he is a good man; in time, he will overcome all his failings. I just know it. This process simply wants time to see its way through and is all the more reason for me to remain by his side."

"But surely you cannot always be at Longbourn, Elizabeth."

"No, not always, but for now. Who knows what the future holds?"

That evening, Fitzwilliam took a family dinner with Elizabeth and her father at Longbourn, and it was late into the night when he was obliged to take his leave. Neither he nor Elizabeth had wanted to be parted from the other, and it was only Mr. Bennet's complaints of wanting the evening to end that persuaded Elizabeth to see Fitzwilliam to the door, with a gentle embrace and an implicit promise to meet each other early the next morning at the break of dawn.

Chapter 23 - Assignation

AN INTENSE, albeit unspoken, desire to explore that morning's destination with Fitzwilliam existed in the secret chambers of Elizabeth's heart. This very notion persisted in her like a fanciful reverie, a whimsical aspiration she scarcely trusted would ever come true. Yet fate had surprised her in the most delightful way, bringing forth the unexpected. Indeed, it was beyond her wildest conjecture that Fitzwilliam Darcy himself would take up residence within the confines of Hertfordshire, his estate lying a mere three miles from the village of Longbourn Village.

While Elizabeth was aware of the Darcys' wealth, she had not comprehended its extent until now. Only in this moment, as she witnessed

Fitzwilliam's ability to purchase an entire estate solely to be near her, did the insignificance of her father's fortune become apparent. This tangible display of Fitzwilliam's affection left no room for doubt—it unveiled the depths of his love.

As they rode horseback, making their way to Oakham Mount, the idyllic spot Elizabeth had stumbled upon during her countless rambles, a sense of anticipation filled the air. After being apart for so long, there was so much to discuss. They dismounted their horses, meticulously securing the reins, and strolled hand in hand toward a secluded copse. Settling beside each other, they began their conversation, their voices carrying the import of unspoken desires and concealed conflicts.

A glimmer of excitement danced in Fitzwilliam's eyes as he reached into his satchel, retrieved a small parcel, and presented it to Elizabeth. Her bright eyes widened in pleasant surprise as she accepted the unexpected gift. "What is this?" she asked, her curiosity piqued.

"I meant to give it to you before you left Pemberley. It was meant to be a going away present, but alas…" Fitzwilliam explained with hints of regret in his voice.

Elizabeth understood the reason behind his disappointment. When he questioned her about leaving Pemberley without waiting for his return or even writing a letter, she bore the burden of a disturbing secret—she had indeed written to him, but Lady Anne must have intercepted the letter. She chose to remain silent, unwilling to be the cause of a rift between mother and son.

How could she reveal to an only son that his mother had taken extraordinary measures to keep Elizabeth's letter hidden from him? The weight of such knowledge was too heavy to bear, and thus she offered no defense on the matter.

Faced with the challenge of concealing Lady Anne's actions, Elizabeth opted for a playful yet tender response. "Who is to say I did not write to you every day and simply chose to tuck the letters away?" Her voice carried a mixture of lightness and affection.

Fitzwilliam's brow furrowed as he searched for an explanation. "Why would you do such a thing?"

"Fitzwilliam, you know me to be a selfish creature. I could not bear the thought of depriving myself of the joy of seeing the emotions flicker across your face as you read my letters," Elizabeth replied, a warm smile gracing her lips.

"Selfish indeed, young lady," Fitzwilliam retorted, a playful glint in his eyes. "But did you consider the anguish I experienced, never receiving a single letter from you? It felt as though you had forgotten me entirely."

A pang of guilt briefly overshadowed Elizabeth's features before she dismissed it. Meeting his gaze, she whispered, "No, Fitzwilliam, I could never forget you." Their eyes locked in an intimate connection, brimming with longing and the ache of separation. It rekindled the passion she had harbored since the tender age of sixteen when she first realized her undying love for him. Shaking herself free from the enchantment, she continued, "Besides, since when is it considered proper for an unmarried young woman to correspond with an unattached young man with whom she is wholly unconnected?"

"If we are so wholly unconnected as you want to suggest, then how do you explain our being here, just the two of us with me completely in your power?" Fitzwilliam countered, mischief lacing his voice.

"Yes, we find ourselves alone now. However, I would not be surprised if Mrs. Eastman were to come trailing along atop Old Nelly any moment," Elizabeth replied.

"Old Nelly?" Fitzwilliam asked.

She nodded. "Yes, my father's field horse. I have no doubt he would gladly spare her for such an occasion as this," Elizabeth explained.

A tinge of disappointment marred Fitzwilliam's countenance. "Your father takes prodigious pride in keeping us apart."

Elizabeth's brows knitted together. "I wish you would not blame my father for my leaving Pemberley, attributing it to his desire to separate the two of us. His wanting me to come here and live with him is truly for the best, as he sees it, and I cannot disagree. I ought to know about my true roots even if I do love you more than I love anyone else in the entire world."

"Elizabeth, love takes many forms and shades, so when you express your love for me as you just did, what are you truly saying?"

Elizabeth peered into her companion's eyes. "Have we not exchanged such sentiments countless times before? I believe you understand precisely what I mean."

Observing her guarded response, Fitzwilliam leaned closer, his voice a mere whisper. "I see you are determined to deflect when it comes to your feelings for me, but let me assure you, my dearest," he said, his eyes never leaving hers. "It is with the greatest sincerity that I tell you my feelings have radically changed since our early days together. I dare not try to hide my true feelings a minute longer," Fitzwilliam confessed.

His words hung in the air, thick with longing and anticipation. And in a moment of unspoken understanding, Fitzwilliam brushed a light, lingering kiss upon Elizabeth's chin—a tender gesture that spoke volumes of his affection.

Chapter 24 - Reservations

THOMAS BENNET HAD WELCOMED his daughter's return home with open arms. Elizabeth's presence breathed life into their house, providing solace amid the lingering pain of losing his wife and their other child. While the ache in his heart would never entirely dissipate, it had certainly lessened.

However, Fitzwilliam Darcy's arrival stirred a mixture of alarm and curiosity within him. The audacity of the young man to purchase the neighboring estate outright! He must have paid a hefty price for the place, considering the previous owner's firm vow never to let go of the estate.

Having young Darcy as his neighbor brought with it a certain expectation. Bennet understood the newcomer was owed a significant amount of respect within their society. He acknowledged this obligation, even as he feared that the gentleman's presence might inadvertently harm Elizabeth. Although the young man had yet to fully inherit his own wealth, Bennet knew he possessed some fortune of his own. Still, he was beholden to his parents. While Bennet's friend, Gerald Darcy, posed no threat to Elizabeth, the same could not be said of Lady Anne Darcy.

Lady Anne Darcy and her ilk countenanced no disappointment, not when it concerned the family's standing in society. They were a proud people whose roots were steeped in the aristocracy. No, she would never allow her son to marry beneath him, despite Lady Anne Darcy raising and caring for Elizabeth as she would have done her own daughter, had she lived.

My Lizzy is not of noble blood. She is not wealthy in her own right. Therefore, in Lady Anne Darcy's eyes, she is not considered worthy of being the next mistress of Pemberley.

The sun had just begun to cast its golden rays across the breakfast room as Elizabeth returned from her invigorating morning outing. The scent of freshly brewed coffee mingled with the aroma of warm pastries, filling the air with an enticing allure. The room exuded a cozy atmosphere, with sunlight filtering through lace curtains, painting delicate patterns on the polished wooden table.

Seated at the head of the table, Mr. Bennet looked up from his newspaper, his curiosity piqued. "What say you about your reunion with young Darcy, Lizzy?" he inquired, his voice laced with genuine interest, eager to delve into the nature of their recent encounter.

Elizabeth's vibrant smile illuminated her face as she responded, "It was entirely unexpected and utterly delightful."

"Not entirely unexpected. Surely you knew beforehand that he was the one who purchased Netherfield Park?" Mr. Bennet asked, raising an eyebrow.

"I suppose when I said our reunion was utterly unexpected, I was referring to his presence here at Longbourn when I returned from my morning calls yesterday," Elizabeth clarified.

"Hmm," was the gentleman's response.

"Papa, I am well aware of your reservations. I shall be mindful of your concerns, but I also have my own reasons. I will not pretend that I am not delighted to spend time in Fitzwilliam's company. I always have been, and that will never change," Elizabeth explained, her voice filled with gentle determination.

"Fitzwilliam?" he asked, his brow furrowing.

Elizabeth paused in her task and regarded her father intently. "How else would you have me refer to the person in this world with whom I am closest?"

"I will offer the same advice to you as I did to the young man himself," he said.

"With all due respect, Papa, I would ask you to spare me. Fitzwilliam and I have already decided how we shall conduct ourselves in the presence of others. I cannot feign indifference between us when I am with you. I cannot always put on pretenses," Elizabeth said, her voice carrying a touch of weariness.

"As long as you are aware of your own intentions, my dear, I must trust you to make the right choices," Mr. Bennet said, a hint of resignation in his tone.

"Trust me, Papa. I know exactly what I am about," Elizabeth said as much for her father's sake as she did for her own.

The lingering pleasure of Fitzwilliam's soft lips against her skin heavy on her mind, Elizabeth picked up her teacup and took a sip, thinking to herself, *Perhaps if I espouse said sentiment often enough, I will begin to believe it myself.*

Chapter 25 - Reflection

Seated within the comforting confines of Longbourn's parlor, Elizabeth and Fitzwilliam found solace in their lively conversation, a delicate interplay between formal propriety and intimate familiarity. Elizabeth's heart and mind were ablaze with curiosity as she sought further insight into the gentleman's intentions.

"Fitzwilliam," she began, her voice adorned with a hint of curiosity, "do you foresee your departure from Hertfordshire in the near future?"

A man of measured words, Fitzwilliam briefly hesitated, his eyes momentarily averted, before he carefully chose his response. His voice filled with tenderness, he said, "The yuletide season swiftly approaches, does it not? Where else would I be if not here with you?"

Elizabeth's brows furrowed. "You might be in Derbyshire, among your family."

"I do not understand," Fitzwilliam replied, a touch of confusion clouding his expression. "Are you not my family, Elizabeth?"

"I meant..." Elizabeth faltered, attempting to clarify her thoughts. "I suppose I meant your immediate relatives in Derbyshire."

"If you are concerned about my being apart from my Derbyshire relations, there is one way to ensure a happy outcome for all of us."

"And what is that?"

"Let us return to Pemberley together—you, me, and your father. I am certain my father would be delighted by such a prospect."

But what of your mother? Elizabeth wondered in silence. *I am sure the sight of the two of us reunited is the last thing Lady Anne would wish to behold.*

"As tempting as your scheme sounds," Elizabeth began, her voice teeming with disappointment—for reasons her companion could not possibly be completely unaware of, "I have already made plans for Christmas. You see, my uncle and aunt Gardiner are planning to come here with their little children. We are meant to have a festive time. I dare not disappoint any of them."

"Christmas in Hertfordshire it shall be then," Fitzwilliam affirmed, his voice resolute. "For I have promised that we shall spend every Christmas together, and I mean to keep all my promises to you."

His declaration stirred a flood of memories within Elizabeth, transporting her back to countless Christmases past. The joyous festivities, the enchantment that seemed to envelop Pemberley during that time of year, and the heartwarming presence of her closest and dearest friend—Fitzwilliam. She cherished those moments, for they held a special place in her heart, reserved solely for him.

Pemberley in December held a distinct allure, different from its summertime splendor. It beckoned them to embark on wintry adventures, exploring the grounds together, their shared bond allowing Elizabeth to indulge in activities that were deemed unbecoming for a young lady. Yet, in Fitzwilliam's presence, Elizabeth was at liberty to enjoy other unmaidenly pursuits, for he was too fond of her to deny her anything she asked of him. Lady Anne was much too doting on her son to criticize him for anything. In her eyes, Fitzwilliam could do no wrong, which indeed benefited the two young people.

As Elizabeth's thoughts drifted, she recalled a particular Christmas when Fitzwilliam had been absent, a year that had deviated from their cherished tradition. The Darcy family had received a letter informing them of Fitzwilliam's decision to spend the season in another county with his friends. Lady Anne had been visibly upset, unable to fathom spending Christmas without her beloved son. However, Elizabeth's disappointment had been far more profound, driving her to retreat to her room seeking solitude. She was always the happiest, most caring person, and she never did anything to cause anyone great concern for her well-being.

Lady Anne was in disbelief. Something had to be done. It was not right that a young girl of sixteen should be so attached to a young man who had friends of his own age who must certainly capture the greatest share of his attention.

Lady Anne had supposed Elizabeth's feelings

for her son were no more than an infatuation born out of familiarity and the convenience of proximity. She attributed any such sentiments she detected on her son's part to his being overprotective and caring. Anything but love. His engagement to Anne de Bourgh in Kent rendered him safe from female entanglements that might otherwise give rise to concern.

Regardless of the affectionate heart Elizabeth must entertain for Fitzwilliam as a result of the preference he always showed her during their years growing up together at Pemberley, her ladyship tried to explain to Elizabeth that he could not always prioritize her.

Though Fitzwilliam was not to return to Derbyshire that December, he promised his family he would join them in London at the start of the year—when Lady Anne's brother, the Earl of Matlock, and his wife held their annual Twelfth Night ball. And although Elizabeth was not yet out in society—having persuaded Lady Anne that she was not yet ready—there was no reason why Elizabeth could not partake in private dinner parties and similar gatherings among family and close acquaintances.

The idea of attending her first ball revived her spirits tenfold. Having accompanied Mr. Darcy and Lady Anne to the Matlocks' home the evening of their Twelfth Night ball with the promise of remaining in the family quarters, Elizabeth, being the curious creature she was, had other intentions. Thus she slipped away from her companion, who had nodded off over a book. Donning the mask she had stashed away, Elizabeth made her way to the ballroom.

She recalled the affair as if it had happened yesterday. The memory of that enchanted evening resurfaced in her mind, transporting her back to a time of youthful indiscretions and stolen moments.

The touch of a gentleman's hand on her shoulder had set her nerves on edge, her thoughts swirling with apprehension over the possibility of being asked to dance. Instinctively, she feigned obliviousness, ignoring the persistent attempts to capture her attention. But then something extraordinary occurred—a warm and tender brush against the side of her face, a sensation that ignited a whirlwind of emotions within her.

Could this be her penance for venturing into the festive gathering without permission, drawing the attention of a gentleman who refused to be disregarded? The thrill of anticipation heightened inside her as he whispered in her ear. "Come with me."

His words resonated with a captivating mix of certainty and mystery. Her heart raced within her chest, the realization dawning upon her that the object of her fascination stood directly behind her. Much too close behind her.

Before Elizabeth could utter a word, he took hold of her arm, leading her swiftly to a secluded part of the house, where a locked door offered them both an escape. They found themselves standing together, hidden from prying eyes, with Fitzwilliam towering over her—his presence both familiar and exhilarating.

"Why am I not surprised to find you here?" he remarked, a hint of amusement dancing in his eyes.

Longing to embrace him, yearning for the affectionate displays they had shared in more innocent times, Elizabeth fought against her desires. This was not Pemberley, where their uninhibited displays of affection were accepted. They were in the heart of London at her first ball, a moment she was not supposed to take part in. Their connection had evolved beyond such unguarded expressions of fondness.

Amid the glow of the fire, their sole source of light, and the distant sounds of revelry, Elizabeth grappled with conflicting emotions. Though her feelings had blossomed, she had no certainty that Fitzwilliam shared the same sentiments, especially after spending her first Christmas without him, a season marked by longing and absence. Yet, she undeniably missed his company, yearning for their familiar companionship.

His presence at that moment was both a delightful surprise and a reminder of their complex circumstances. Elizabeth attempted to inject a bit of space between them, seeking refuge near a sofa. "This is hardly your element, Fitzwilliam," she commented, her tone laced with playfulness and longing. "I imagine you would much prefer to be at Darcy House, by the fireplace, engrossed in a good book, perhaps savoring a glass of cognac."

Drawing nearer, Fitzwilliam took her hand in his, offering a gentle squeeze. "And yet, here I am," he said. "Upon my arrival at Darcy House, I was informed of your presence here at Matlock House with my parents. How could I possibly stay away, knowing you as I do? I knew you would never confine yourself to the solitude of your apartment, not when such diversions beckoned outside your door, promising the allure of anonymity."

Elizabeth's concerns rose to the surface as she considered the potential repercussions of their *impromptu escapade.* "Are you planning to tell Lady Anne?" *she asked, her voice tinged with worry.*

Fitzwilliam's tender grip tightened. "Have I ever betrayed your confidence, Elizabeth?" *he replied, his voice comforting.*

"No," *she admitted, a flicker of relief crossing her features.* "But this is different from the mischief-making I often engage in at home. Lady Anne would be beside herself if she discovered I had ventured into society before my formal debut, even in disguise. You know how she would react."

"Fear not, my dear. Your secret is secure. Speaking of secrets, there is a reason I brought you here. I have the means to return you to where you ought to be without the risk of being detected."

Elizabeth's eyes lit up with excitement. "A secret passage perhaps?" *she asked. She adored their little adventures together, the thrill of clandestine discoveries.*

Fitzwilliam nodded, his eyes filled with anticipation. "Come with me," *he beckoned, his voice carrying a sense of intrigue.*

Elizabeth hesitated, a mix of emotions coursing through her. She yearned to prolong their time together, reluctant to part ways so soon. After all, they were in London, a city bustling with diversions that could easily captivate a young man's attention.

"If your concern is my imminent departure," Fitzwilliam said, sensing her hesitation, "fear not. I have no intention of leaving you just yet."

Relieved, Elizabeth dismissed her reservations, acknowledging her unfounded worries. "I suppose I am being foolish," she confessed. "No doubt you have plans for the evening, surrounded by friends and acquaintances. It is Twelfth Night after all, a night filled with mystery, wonder, and other subjects I perhaps should not mention."

Fitzwilliam chuckled. "I believe someone has indulged in too much reading," he teased.

"And whose fault is that? I am sure I would not spend nearly so much time reading as I do were it not for your inclination to do the same. Besides, have you not always told me that one can never enjoy too much of what is good for them? And nothing is better for a person's soul than reading."

"Then I suppose you ought to be thanking me, for I am of the opinion that the epitome of an accomplished woman is one who is constantly improving her mind through extensive reading."

Fitzwilliam laced his fingers with Elizabeth's and drew her hand closer. "I am happy to accompany you to one of the sitting rooms and read with you for a while."

"You would do that for me?"

"You ought to know by now there is nothing I would not do for you."

Elizabeth pulled her hand away. "Nothing besides coming home for Christmas," she said.

He met her gaze, a sincere apology in his eyes. "I am sorry if my absence during the Christmas season disappointed you, Elizabeth," he expressed with genuine remorse. "I never wish to deny you anything that brings you happiness."

A tinge of sadness tugged at Elizabeth's heart. "We have never spent Christmas apart since we first met," she said, the agony of their long separation evident in her voice.

Understanding the depth of her longing, Fitzwilliam sought to make amends. "Then let me make a promise," he declared. "We shall never spend Christmas apart from each other again."

A playful glint entered Elizabeth's eyes as she seized the opportunity to tease him, fully aware of his mother's intentions for his future. "I mean it, Fitzwilliam. You, me ... and your cousin Anne," she quipped.

Fitzwilliam cast a perturbed glance over his

shoulder before returning to her. "What am I to do with you?" he asked, a mix of exasperation and affection lacing his words.

Elizabeth knew he did not like to be teased about his mother's plans for his future marriage to Miss Anne de Bourgh. He rarely liked to be teased under any circumstances, and she was one of the few people he allowed to get away with it. How could she possibly resist such an irresistible temptation? He had told her often enough that his mother's wishes were not his. Still, Elizabeth rather supposed that until he shared his opinion with his mother, she was at liberty to taunt him all the same.

"You did mention making amends," she said.

"Indeed. What do you say to my spending every spare moment entertaining you until I leave town?"

"Let me see..." she began, placing a finger to her chin in contemplation. "Make that every waking moment and I shall accept your proposal."

A smile played at Fitzwilliam's lips as he acquiesced. "Every waking moment it is," he agreed, his voice filled with warmth. "I am, as ever, your humble servant."

. . .

Recalling herself to the present, Elizabeth was delighted knowing Fitzwilliam meant to keep his promise to spend every Christmas with her. A troubling thought entered her mind. Yes, he was there now, but what about the next year or the year after that? Sooner or later, his familial duties would surely call, thus separating the two of them—perhaps forever.

I will not worry about that now. I prefer instead to embrace this time I have with Fitzwilliam and cherish it in my heart forever.

Elizabeth smiled. She was delighted by the prospect of being with him, but the chance to tease him was too tempting to let pass. "How wonderful! Shall I write to invite your cousin Anne too or is her presence not deemed necessary until after—"

He placed a finger on Elizabeth's lips to hush her. "Do not dare speak another word on the subject, young lady. Otherwise, I shall have to take more drastic measures to quieten you."

Elizabeth's heart melted as her busy mind tried to envision the sort of measures he had in mind. Even if unintentionally cast, the spell he had over her was immediately broken when he lowered his finger from her lips.

Elizabeth felt disappointment and relief as they broke eye contact and he turned and left the room. She wondered if they would always be engaged in this dance of emotions, knowing that any hope she secretly harbored of him sharing her love would likely never come to fruition.

Not as long as Lady Anne's avowed disapproval stands in our way.

Chapter 26 - Explanation

FITZWILLIAM AND ELIZABETH walked along the bustling streets of Meryton, their steps matching the lively rhythm of the surrounding atmosphere. As they rounded a corner, they caught sight of Lieutenant Wickham. The chance encounter presented the perfect opportunity for Elizabeth to reconnect the long-lost acquaintances and satisfy her curiosity about Wickham's past association with Pemberley.

"Come, Fitzwilliam! There is a most amiable gentleman whom I have recently befriended and am eager to introduce to you," she exclaimed, her eyes brimming with anticipation.

Fitzwilliam arched an eyebrow, revealing his reluctance. "Surely you jest, Elizabeth. You know how much I detest engaging in small talk with those with whom I am not intimately acquainted."

Elizabeth linked her arm through his. "Hence your well-earned reputation as the *Recluse of Netherfield Park*," she teased, referring to his tendency to avoid mingling with his neighbors. "However, in this case, I will not allow you to stand around looking stupid while I engage in the obligatory pleasantries. Besides, this particular person boasts of a connection to your family, rendering your excuse futile."

With determination, she practically pulled Fitzwilliam across the street until they reached Lieutenant Wickham, who was conversing with another officer. The other officer tipped his hat and quickly stepped away, leaving only the three of them.

"Miss Bennet." Wickham greeted Elizabeth with a charming smile. "What a delight to see you on such a fine day."

"The pleasure is entirely mine, sir." Elizabeth glanced away from Mr. Wickham and turned to Fitzwilliam. "Allow me to introduce my dear friend, Mr. Fitzwilliam Darcy. Or rather reintroduce you, for I believe your acquaintance goes back many years."

Both gentlemen nodded in acknowledgment.

"It has been quite a while since we last saw each other," George Wickham remarked.

"Indeed," Fitzwilliam concurred, feeling the awkwardness of the circumstances.

Despite playing together as children, the two were very different in temperament. Wickham had often been described as wild, but Fitzwilliam could not help but question the validity of such characterizations, considering they primarily stemmed from his mother. Lady Anne believed that no one was worthy of her beloved son, leading Fitzwilliam to wonder if her negative opinion of Wickham was influenced by his inferior social standing compared to that of the Darcys. His mother's sentiments were echoed by other members of the Fitzwilliam family, especially his aunt, Lady Catherine de Bourgh.

Nevertheless, Fitzwilliam had indeed regarded Wickham as a friend. He was the only person close to his age in the vicinity of Pemberley, excluding the children of some of the servants who dared not approach the young master. Young Darcy did not let on how disappointed he was upon returning to Pemberley from Matlock one day all those years ago to find that George Wickham was gone—that

Wickham's grandfather had arrived and removed the young boy from Derbyshire to live with him hundreds of miles away in another county. Since then, Fitzwilliam and Wickham had not crossed paths until that day.

The conversation between the three soon turned mundane, with Wickham and Elizabeth engaged in small talk while Fitzwilliam endured the exchange. After consulting his pocket watch, Fitzwilliam interrupted, aware of their impending dinner plans. "Miss Bennet, if we are to return to Longbourn in time to dine with your father, we ought to take our leave."

Once they had parted from Wickham, Elizabeth confronted Fitzwilliam about his seemingly ill-mannered behavior toward his childhood friend. "I demand an account for your ungentlemanly behavior," she said, a mix of curiosity and reproach in her tone.

Fitzwilliam sighed, realizing he owed her an account of his actions. "As I can never deny you anything, I shall fully explain my history with Mr. Wickham. Once you hear what I have to say, you will understand that my behavior was not ungentlemanly."

When Fitzwilliam had finished confiding in

Elizabeth his past with George Wickham, he concluded, "Though, before today, I have not seen Wickham in years. I recall, however, hearing that he turned out very bad, a gamester and a rake, leading me to insist that you keep your distance from him."

Despite Fitzwilliam's annoyingly officious stance on whom she should and should not spend her time with, his explanation perfectly aligned with Wickham's story. Unfortunately, this confirmation gave Elizabeth more discomfort than pleasure. It was another example of the lengths Lady Anne went to in efforts to shield her son from those she deemed not worthy enough for Pemberley's heir. It did not escape her notice that Fitzwilliam did not mention Lady Anne's part in Wickham's exile from Pemberley, which made her wonder if he even knew his mother.

Not that I am the one to enlighten him on his mother's deficits. Some matters are best left unspoken, she reminded herself.

"I have dined with Mr. Wickham on numerous occasions," Elizabeth said, coming to Wickham's defense. "He has been a guest at Longbourn and is well liked by my neighbors and acquaintances. I have seen no evidence to support your assertions."

Fitzwilliam's tone grew serious as he tried to convey his concerns. "And what of it? Consider yourself fortunate and heed my warning to keep it that way."

"I do not appreciate your officious attitude, Fitzwilliam. In this case, perhaps I shall rely on my own judgment."

Fitzwilliam's voice softened. "Do you remember when you used to get frightened after reading about monsters, despite your insistence on doing so anyway?"

Elizabeth nodded, a smile playing on her lips. She recalled a particular book and how Fitzwilliam had spent hours comforting her until she drifted off to sleep.

"You must recall my promise that I would never allow the monsters to come near you."

A mischievous glint appeared in Elizabeth's eyes. "Are you implying that Lieutenant Wickham is a monster and you intend to protect me from him?"

"It is not merely about protecting you from Wickham. The truth is I do not want him or any gentleman of his kind anywhere near you."

Elizabeth's teasing smile remained. "It sounds

like someone is experiencing a severe bout of jealousy."

"Jealousy, Elizabeth?" Fitzwilliam asked, his eyes locked with hers.

She nodded. "Why else would you be so concerned?"

"If you choose to dismiss my concerns as jealousy, then so be it. As long as you heed my counsel, I shall have no cause for concern."

Their eyes locked, the world around them fading into insignificance as a surge of undeniable passion passed between them. Elizabeth never wished to be at odds with Fitzwilliam for too long. She swallowed. "On the other hand, there is something to be said about jealousy so long as it is under good regulation."

"Under good regulation indeed. It is not without its advantages," he whispered.

Elizabeth's heart skipped a beat. "Then, my dearest companion, may I forever be the cause of your delightful, well-regulated jealousy."

Chapter 27 - Consolation

Fitzwilliam Darcy had just finished his breakfast when the rhythmic sound of a horse trotting down the drive filled the air, pulling him out of his thoughts. His brow furrowed in wonder as he left the breakfast room and stepped outside. His eyes followed the long, winding drive that led to the house. Through the morning mist, he spotted the figure of a familiar rider on horseback, his cousin, Colonel Fitzwilliam.

The young master was completely caught off guard, though he welcomed his cousin's arrival. A couple years older than Fitzwilliam, the colonel was the second son of the Earl of Matlock. The two men were as close as could be, more like brothers than first cousins—though Fitzwilliam had never told the colonel as much. In stark contrast to Fitzwilliam's reserved nature, the colonel had a gregarious demeanor. There was a certain charm about him that put people at ease, enabling him to slide seamlessly into conversations with everyone he encountered, be it an old acquaintance or a new face. He was a master at bridging differences.

Fitzwilliam was not simply reserved. Many, including his new neighbors, deemed him haughty. Not that he could be bothered by what those wholly unconnected to him thought.

The gentlemen commenced greeting each other in accordance with their standing as relations and friends.

"Cousin, this is quite an impressive estate you have acquired," the colonel remarked, beholding the sweeping surroundings with admiration. "It is not at all like the other properties in your growing portfolio. But why Hertfordshire of all places?"

Fitzwilliam hesitated, unsure how to respond. He knew that explaining his true motivations would reveal his intentions, which he was not yet ready to disclose. After a brief internal struggle, he settled for a simple answer.

"I have my reasons," he said, his voice infused with quiet determination. The colonel nodded knowingly, a silent understanding passing between them as they retreated indoors.

As they entered the grand drawing room, Fitzwilliam sensed his cousin's inquisitive eyes fixed upon him. He could tell that the colonel suspected his true motive in acquiring Netherfield Park, surmising his intentions toward a certain young lady. He decided it was time to address the unspoken question, clearing his throat before speaking.

"What harm is there in owning a country estate conveniently located near town?" Fitzwilliam asked, turning to face his cousin directly.

A knowing smile played on the colonel's lips as he responded in a playful yet perceptive tone, "If you consider a half day's travel convenient."

"Under good road conditions, a half day's travel poses no inconvenience," Fitzwilliam countered, asserting his stance. "Besides, there are other inducements that have led me to this property, and you can be in no doubt as to what I am speaking of—or rather whom."

Colonel Fitzwilliam's amusement was evident as he replied, "I have not the faintest idea."

"Come now, Cousin. Am I to pretend that my mother did not send you here to do her bidding?"

"Lady Anne?"

"I have only one mother. Lady Anne is a very strong-willed woman, and she will always do what she believes is best for her family. In this case, that means keeping Elizabeth and me as far apart as possible."

"So, you have your mother's character all figured out," the colonel said, raising an eyebrow.

Fitzwilliam sighed, well aware of the extent of his mother's manipulations. "She only just accepted that I will never marry Anne before she began presenting me with a list of potential brides, hoping I would choose one among them. But given my unwavering desire to be here in Hertfordshire, close to Elizabeth, it is an unlikely prospect."

"Why not simply propose to Elizabeth and put an end to Lady Anne's machinations? You must know that is the only thing that will stop her."

Fitzwilliam's expression softened, his thoughts overtaken by the woman who held his heart. "I do not wish to rush Elizabeth into something she may not be ready for. It is important for her to rebuild her relationship with her father, and

I do not want to hinder her efforts in any way. I will wait for her."

"Spoken like a man who is truly confident in his position. Who is to say Elizabeth will ever go against your mother's favorite wish to see you marry a woman with her own fortune, one with status, connections, and, if possible, noble blood coursing through her veins?"

Fitzwilliam chuckled dryly. "I am not blind to the realities of our situation or the challenges we face. Going against my mother's desires and causing her pain is the last thing Elizabeth would want. But she is the only woman I desire, and I believe she feels the same way about me as I feel about her. Her words, actions, and mere presence speak to me in ways no other woman's ever has. I know she is the one for me, and I am willing to wait as long as it takes to make her mine."

"I suppose the next thing you will tell me is Elizabeth has bewitched you, body and soul."

"I dare say she has."

The colonel smiled, admiration and support evident in his face. "Very well, Cousin. I stand by you in your pursuit, as I always have. But do not be surprised if your mother attempts to interfere once more."

The younger man nodded. His dark eyes gleamed with determination. "I understand the power of Elizabeth's reverence for my mother and the challenges it presents. I have to believe that time will allow her to see that what we share is meant to be—more powerful than the feelings of others. I will continue to court her in secret and love her unconditionally, regardless of the obstacles that lie in our path. I cannot fathom a life without her by my side. Elizabeth is my heart and soul, and I will do whatever it takes for the two of us to be together."

"I have no doubt that you will face any obstacle with unwavering resolve, Cousin," the colonel said, placing a reassuring hand on the younger man's shoulder. "Your resilience and steadfast enthusiasm are truly admirable."

Fitzwilliam's grateful smile mirrored his cousin's words as they fell into a comfortable silence, each lost in their own contemplations. He knew that the road ahead would be arduous, with his mother's interference and societal expectations working against him. Nevertheless, he was determined to fight for what he wanted.

Elizabeth Bennet is worth every challenge and sacrifice. She is all I want, no matter the cost.

SIMPLY BEAUTIFUL

The colonel looked at his cousin, a mischievous glimmer dancing in his eyes. "About the litany of bridal prospects your mother painstakingly prepared. Would you care to divulge the details?"

Fitzwilliam arched his brow. "Why ever would you ask such an absurd question, Cousin?"

He chuckled, leaning back in his chair. "It seems you have forgotten my predicament. Unlike you, the fortunate heir to Pemberley, I am but a second son. Given my brother's robust health and his secure position as the viscount, my extravagant habits force me into a dependent situation. The lure of a list of young heiresses is far too appealing to resist."

Fitzwilliam shook his head. The colonel's frequent complaints on the subject always had a way of resurfacing. "Alas, I fear I will not be of any help in your quest, Cousin. I consigned my mother's officiously crafted list to the flames under her watchful eye."

The older gentleman scoffed, his mirthful eyes shining with unspoken laughter. "Of course you did."

Fitzwilliam shrugged. "Why on earth would I

hold on to such a thing given where my heart lies?"

The colonel held up his hand. "Say no more." Standing to stretch his long legs, he said, "Since we have exhausted the subject on matters of the heart, what say you give me a proper tour of this advantageously located estate you have acquired? And perhaps, once we have explored all the best parts of Netherfield Park, we can pay a visit to Elizabeth. It has been far too long since I last saw the young lady who holds your heart in her palm."

Chapter 28 - Determination

Weeks later, Elizabeth and Fitzwilliam found themselves meandering through the serene meadows, bathed in the soft glow of the rising sun. As they strolled to a stop, the soft trill of birds chirping filled the air around them. Fitzwilliam's gaze rested on Elizabeth, his eyes filled with intensity, causing her heart to flutter in response.

"You have been rather somber this morning as if you are carrying the weight of the world on your shoulders. May I ask what is on your mind?" Elizabeth asked softly.

Fitzwilliam paused, taking a deep breath to steady himself. "There is something important I wish to discuss with you. It should go without saying, but I feel compelled to express it. I love you, Elizabeth—most ardently. I have loved you for as long as I can remember—only you. I do not wish to rush you, but I cannot envision a life without you. The time has come for us to start discussing our future ... as husband and wife."

Elizabeth regarded him intently. "Surely you must know your mother will never accept me as your wife. Eventually, societal pressures will force you to choose a woman from your own sphere—a union driven by wealth and influence, if not with your cousin Anne then with someone else."

"No, Elizabeth. I refuse to betray myself in such a manner. And I certainly will not betray you."

"But that is precisely the point, Fitzwilliam. By marrying within your own sphere, you would merely conform to the expectations imposed by your family and society," Elizabeth said.

"And what about you, Elizabeth? Should I expect you to do the same? To wed solely to fulfill societal expectations?" Fitzwilliam asked, his eyes searching hers.

"No, Fitzwilliam. Not at all. I will marry for love or I will not marry at all," Elizabeth declared with unwavering conviction.

"Then let us make a pact, Elizabeth. Let us vow

that we shall both marry for love or neither of us shall marry at all," Fitzwilliam proposed, a glimmer of hope in his eyes.

"Agreed," Elizabeth said, a hint of a smile playing on her lips.

Fitzwilliam continued, "And since we are already in love, I suppose we should marry."

"Oh? But who said I am already in love?" Elizabeth teased.

In a swift motion, Fitzwilliam took her hand and brought it to his lips, bestowing a tender kiss upon her knuckles. He then locked his eyes with hers. "Are you not, Elizabeth?"

Elizabeth felt her knees weaken slightly, causing her to withdraw her hand slowly. "You are quite incorrigible," she said playfully, before turning to walk away.

His mouth agape, Fitzwilliam stood there watching Elizabeth's retreating figure, his heart racing with anticipation. He had revealed his most heartfelt sentiments, laying all his cards on the table, and this was her response.

He could not believe it. Was it possible that Elizabeth did not reciprocate his love? Had he made a mistake by confessing his feelings and suggesting they get married too soon? He had to know.

"Elizabeth," he called out, quickening his pace to catch up with her. "Wait."

She turned around, her expression a mosaic of curiosity and confusion. "What is it, Fitzwilliam?"

"I need to know," he began, his voice filled with a mix of hope and vulnerability. "Do you feel the same way I do?"

Elizabeth hesitated, her eyes searching his face for a timeless moment. Then, she softly uttered, "Yes, Fitzwilliam. I love you."

Relief surged through Fitzwilliam, lifting the weight from his shoulders. He reached for her hand once more, drawing her near. "Then marry me, Elizabeth. Let us begin our lives together as one."

Elizabeth's face fell, a trace of sadness clouding her features. "I cannot marry you, Fitzwilliam."

He was taken aback, his eyes wide with confusion. "What do you mean? Why not?"

"It is because of your mother. Lady Anne opposes a union between us. Before I left Pemberley, she made her disapproval abundantly clear. She believes I am not a suitable match for you," Elizabeth revealed, her voice evidencing with disappointment.

Fitzwilliam's heart sank at her words. Would he be forced to choose between his love for Elizabeth and his family? The mere thought of such a predicament was agonizing.

"But I love you, Elizabeth," he said. "I can no longer fathom a life without you as my wife."

"I know," Elizabeth whispered tenderly. "And I love you too. But I cannot disregard your mother's wishes. Not after everything she has done for me. It would not be fair to her or to us."

An anguished knot twisted in Fitzwilliam's stomach. Elizabeth's reasoning was rational, yet it did little to alleviate the pain of their circumstances. His voice filled with a mixture of desperation and longing, he asked, "What are we to do then?"

Elizabeth peered up at him, her eyes shimmering with unshed tears. "I do not know, Fitzwilliam. Truly, I do not."

They stood there, enveloped in a poignant silence, each lost in their own thoughts. Fitzwilliam understood that he could not force

Elizabeth into marriage, yet the prospect of a life without her seemed unfathomable.

"I will speak with my mother. I am confident that I can persuade her to see reason."

Elizabeth looked at him, her eyes a blend of hope and skepticism. "Do you truly believe it is possible?"

Fitzwilliam hesitated for a moment, unsure of his own words. At length, he peered into Elizabeth's eyes, armed with resolute conviction. "I will do whatever it takes to make you mine, Elizabeth. I will fight for us."

Elizabeth's heart swelled with affection for Fitzwilliam. Never before had she felt so loved and cherished. Yet, alongside that love, fear gripped her. The thought of defying Lady Anne Darcy's wishes was daunting.

"Please, Fitzwilliam, exercise caution," she implored, her voice barely a whisper. "I do not want you to do anything that could harm your relationship with your mother."

Fitzwilliam nodded. "I understand, Elizabeth. However, I cannot allow our love to be destroyed by my mother's prejudices. I will employ every means at my disposal to make her see that you are the woman with whom I plan to share my life."

He reached out and gently brushed his fingers against Elizabeth's cheek, a gesture filled with tenderness and affection. "I promise you, Elizabeth, that I will not give up on us. Our love is worth fighting for, even if it means battling against my own flesh and blood."

Elizabeth's eyes softened, and a smile graced her lips. She placed her hand over his, pressing it against her cheek, savoring their connection. At that moment, the world around them faded into insignificance, leaving only the two of them—bound by an unbreakable bond.

Fitzwilliam leaned in and tenderly kissed Elizabeth—his lips caressing hers with warmth and affection. It was a kiss that conveyed his abiding love, his longing, and a promise that no sacrifice was too much, and no struggle too insurmountable to keep them apart.

The love they shared was a force that transcended circumstances—a love that was meant to be.

Chapter 29 - Consternation

Fitzwilliam received word of his parents' imminent arrival in Hertfordshire mere hours after he had sent his own letter to Lady Anne. The anticipation weighed heavily on him as he paced nervously in the front hall of Netherfield, waiting anxiously for his parents to arrive. It had been months since he had last seen them and he could not help but wonder how they would react to his sudden purchase of the estate in Hertfordshire. While he knew they had been disappointed in his lack of progress in securing a suitable marriage, he hoped they would ultimately be proud of his independent actions in acquiring Netherfield.

Finally, the familiar sound of rattling wheels and the clip-clop of hooves announced the arrival of the carriage. Fitzwilliam hurried to the door, his heart pounding in his chest. Stepping onto the front steps, he caught sight of his father descending from the carriage. Tall and imposing in his traveling attire, the elder Mr. Darcy commanded attention wherever he went. Following closely behind was Lady Anne, her elegant figure draped in a cloak of dark, regal silk. Fitzwilliam's apprehension grew as he prepared to greet his parents, a mix of excitement and trepidation swirling within him. While his father's stern expression always made him slightly anxious, he held a deep respect for the man whose expectations loomed large in his life. On the other hand, Lady Anne was a warm and affectionate woman, quick to embrace her son. Her nurturing nature had always provided him with solace and comfort.

As they entered the grand foyer of Netherfield, Fitzwilliam paused, allowing his parents to take in the splendor of the recently refurbished estate. Countless hours of hard work had gone into restoring Netherfield to its full glory, and he hoped that his parents would approve of his efforts. His father wasted no time in appraising the property with a discerning eye, and Fitzwilliam mentally prepared himself for any criticism that might come his way.

However, to his surprise, a hint of approval softened his father's expression. "Impressive," he murmured, his eyes sweeping across the high ceilings and ornate furnishings. "You have indeed done well for yourself, Fitzwilliam."

Pride surged within Fitzwilliam and a wide grin spread across his face as he glanced at his beaming mother. "Thank you, Father," he responded, his voice filled with emotion. "Your approval means the world to me."

His father's response, though characteristically understated with a mere nod, held deep significance for Fitzwilliam. He knew that his father's praise was not easily given, and he felt a profound sense of satisfaction at having garnered it.

The Darcys did not plan to extend their visit at Netherfield as pressing business affairs in London awaited the older gentleman's attention. The following morning, after spending considerable time reviewing Netherfield's financial records and offering guidance on property management, the elder Mr. Darcy expressed his desire to visit his old friend, Thomas Bennet.

. . .

After riding horseback three miles to the neighboring estate and spending a quarter of an hour with his old friend, the elder Mr. Darcy said, "I thought I might persuade you to ride out with me. I have never had the pleasure of seeing your estate, Bennet. Perhaps you could show me around?"

Mr. Bennet nodded, an intrigued smile playing at the corners of his mouth. "Of course, my dear friend. I would be delighted to show you around Longbourn. It is not often that we receive visitors of your stature here in our little corner of the world."

The two men mounted their horses and set off at a leisurely pace, relishing the crisp air and the picturesque views of Longbourn Village. Mr. Bennet could not help but feel a surge of excitement, knowing that his daughter's return had brought about remarkable changes. He could not have been prouder of her role in the transformation as well as his own.

As they rode side by side beyond the outskirts of Longbourn Village, enjoying the scenic Hertfordshire countryside, there was an unspoken understanding between the two fathers. As much as he enjoyed riding with his friend, there were other factors that stirred Bennet's enthusiasm, for if there was anyone who could sort through the tangled web that his daughter and young Fitzwilliam Darcy were spinning it was the young man's father—the one who controlled the Darcy purse strings as it were.

After listening to Bennet's complaints about the perverse closeness between their children and their obliviousness to society's norms and expectations, Mr. Darcy said, "As much as I might wish to be of service to you, my friend, I do not think I ought to interfere in my son's choices. I have instilled in him the types of values and principles he ought to exercise as a young man and the future heir of Pemberley, but more than that, I have tried to teach him to be his own man. I mean to support the decisions he makes in life, even if they are in direct opposition to the decisions I might make. Surely you can appreciate my stance."

"Ordinarily I would not ask you to interfere in this way. My daughter is my closest remaining relation. Surely you can understand my stance in not wanting to see her hurt?"

"Our children are too sensible to do anything

that is not in their best interests," said the other man.

"If only I could be as certain as you. But what is good for the male species is not necessarily the best for the female."

"I wish you would not worry so much on that front. My son is an excellent young man. He will not wish to do anything that places Elizabeth's heart in jeopardy."

Mr. Bennet sighed, his gaze drifting over the Hertfordshire landscape. "Having witnessed their interactions rather frequently since your son's arrival, I must admit that I believe Fitzwilliam cares deeply for my Lizzy. My concerns lie more with what will happen when his duty to his family beckons."

Mr. Darcy looked out over the sprawling landscape, lost in thought. He knew all too well the magnitude of duty that came with being the heir to a great estate, and he had no illusions about the challenges that lay ahead for his son and his chosen bride. With a wistful smile, he responded, "Ah, duty—a burden shared by all men of our station. But I have faith that Fitzwilliam will fulfill his obligations to Pemberley while also pursuing his own happiness. Bennet, I understand your concerns, but if Fitzwilliam believes that Elizabeth is the one for him, then I will support his decision. And if that means putting his love for her before his duty to Pemberley, then so be it."

Mr. Bennet nodded thoughtfully, his expression reflecting a mix of appreciation and apprehension. "You possess great wisdom, Darcy. I only hope that Elizabeth possesses the strength and resilience to face the challenges that lie ahead. She is a remarkable young woman, but I fear she may find herself in over her head."

Reaching over and placing a reassuring hand on his friend's shoulder, Mr. Darcy offered a warm smile. "I have no doubt that Elizabeth is more than capable of navigating any challenges that come her way. And should she ever need assistance, she will have the unwavering support of the Darcy family."

With those comforting words, the two men fell into a companionable silence, continuing their ride through the idyllic countryside. With each passing minute, the elder Mr. Darcy could not help but feel a sense of satisfaction at having fulfilled his duty as a father, both in terms of guiding his son and supporting his choices and in offering comfort and reassurance to his friend about the future of their children's relationship.

As they approached Longbourn, the silhouette of Fitzwilliam and Elizabeth walking together in the distance came into view. Their heads were bent in deep conversation, an intimate connection evident between them. The elder Mr. Darcy could not help but smile, a swell of paternal pride and joy welling up within him. They were young, they were in love, and in that moment, there was nothing more beautiful in the world.

"Shall we join them, Bennet?" Mr. Darcy proposed, gesturing toward the couple.

Mr. Bennet inclined his head slightly, amusement twinkling in his eyes. "Indeed," he said, playing along with a hint of reserved gravity. "It seems that my primary employment in life is to rein in the impetuosity of the young."

Chapter 30 - Contemplation

While the husband's primary objective was visiting his son in Hertfordshire and spending time with his old friend before journeying on to London, his wife had her own motives.

Lady Anne had arrived in Hertfordshire determined to persuade her beloved son, Fitzwilliam, to travel with them to London. She could not bear the notion of such an extraordinary young man as the heir to Pemberley idling about in an insignificant country estate. She believed that he had been idle for too long and needed to start thinking about his future.

As she gracefully swept into the drawing room later that day, the gentle rustle of her silk gown filled the air, creating a whispering symphony of elegance. The room itself exuded a timeless charm, with its plush furnishings, ornate tapestries, and delicate porcelain figurines adorning the mantelpiece. A crackling fire in the hearth cast a warm and inviting glow that illuminated the refined atmosphere. The scent of lavender hung in the air, its subtle fragrance invoking a sense of tranquility.

Fitzwilliam, who had been engrossed in a book in a quiet corner, raised his head at the sound of his mother's arrival. Surprise flickered in his eyes as he took in her determined expression. Lady Anne wasted no time, her steps purposeful and measured as she closed the distance between them. Her voice, filled with a restrained urgency, cut through the stillness of the room.

"Fitzwilliam, my dear son, I believe it is time for you to come to London with your parents. Whether you agree, we know what is best for you and your future standing in society. You have been here for far too long, and I fear you are squandering your future."

Her words hung in the air, and Fitzwilliam sat there in silence, barely containing his irritation at her officiousness. He had been biding his time, waiting for the right moment to speak with her. It was just as well that his mother had been the one to start their long-delayed conversation, but he was not sure she would like how it would end.

He raised an eyebrow and regarded her with a mixture of curiosity and annoyance. "And what do you suggest I do in London, Mother?"

"You should start courting the daughter of a peer. If you truly do not intend to marry Anne, then you should begin considering your future place among society," Lady Anne responded quickly, her words flowing with an air of authority.

Fitzwilliam's shoulders slumped and a heavy sigh escaped his lips. He understood his mother's intentions but could not bring himself to comply. "Why would I waste my time courting someone merely to appease you and Father when my heart already belongs to another?"

"Dare I ask with whom you believe yourself to be in love?" her ladyship asked.

Fitzwilliam's determined eyes met hers. "Do I really have to say, Mother?" he asked, sweeping his fingers through his hair. "You know me too well to pretend you are unaware of who holds my heart."

Lady Anne hesitated, carefully weighing her words before responding. "How can you be certain that what you feel for Elizabeth is not merely a result of never giving yourself the chance to be with anyone other than her? Similarly, you have denied Elizabeth the opportunity to meet and fall in love with another. The least you can do is consider pursuing others—young ladies of your own sphere."

He shook his head resolutely. "No, Mother, you must understand. My love for Elizabeth consumes every fiber of my being. She is my heart and soul. I can no longer imagine a life without her as my wife. I am resolved to marry her. I will remain unwed for eternity if I cannot have her."

He paused, his heart heavy with the gravity of his words, before continuing with a deep, shuddering breath. "Elizabeth cherishes you as a daughter cherishes a mother. Her selfless love for you prevents her from accepting my proposal. She refuses to disappoint you, Mother. Can you not see her sacrifice—the strength of her love and devotion?"

Fitzwilliam pleaded with his eyes, searching hers for even a glimmer of understanding. "If only you had known, Mother. If you had known that Elizabeth was the woman who would capture my heart and become my wife, would you not have taken her in? Would you not have raised her as your own, showering her with the love and care only a mother can give?"

Silence hung heavy in the air, every second feeling like an eternity as Fitzwilliam anxiously awaited Lady Anne's response. And then, with an air of stoic determination, she said, "No, my dear son, I dare say I would not have changed a thing."

Her words pierced his wounded heart. "Such a revelation only reveals the depth of your love for her. Yet, Mother, why do you persist in standing as an insurmountable barrier between the two of us? Why do you choose to deny us the chance at happiness?" Fitzwilliam asked, his voice trembling as he desperately tried to comprehend her answer.

"I have my reasons, Son," she said, her voice laden with the solemnness of her own hidden sorrows and secrets, leaving Fitzwilliam with a chasm of unanswered questions and uncertain sentiments.

An uneasy feeling washed over him as he tore his eyes away from his beloved mother's face. Deep down, he feared his decision to take Elizabeth as his wife would irreparably damage their relationship. However, frustration simmered within him as he realized Lady Anne had no intention of relenting from her disapproval. Clearly, Lady Anne's refusal was far more complicated than what initially appeared on the surface.

Realizing that further discussion would be futile, Fitzwilliam glared at his mother. "When you find yourself estranged from your only son and wonder why, remember that I, too, have my reasons."

With those words, Fitzwilliam turned away from his mother and walked toward the door. His heart yearned to escape the tension-filled atmosphere of the room. But before he could reach the exit, Lady Anne's voice broke the silence. "Son, wait—"

Chapter 31 - Confession

THE NEXT DAY, Lady Anne planned to call on Elizabeth at Longbourn. At last, she had awakened to the fact that she had underestimated the bond between the young lady and her son. After a light breakfast, she embarked on the brief journey from Netherfield Park to the neighboring estate.

Upon arriving at the grounds of Longbourn, a small yet efficient staff greeted her, and she soon found herself in the front parlor of the Bennet home.

She knew it was foolish to be so nervous, yet the harsh memories of the infamous Pemberley debacle still haunted her. Observing the family's prominently displayed portrait brought those thoughts rushing back. Studying Mrs. Bennet's face, Lady Anne realized she would never forget their last exchange at Pemberley all those years ago. She also acknowledged, with a pang of regret, that she undoubtedly would if she had a chance to take those words back.

The ticking clock drew her attention to the fact that Elizabeth had not yet appeared, heightening her worry. She had not seen Elizabeth since that fateful day at Pemberley and was aware that no warm welcome was guaranteed.

She steadied her trembling hands and savored the solitude, knowing that their relationship would be forever altered when the formidable reunion finally occurred. The warm embrace that greeted her when Elizabeth entered the room was unexpected but welcome.

"Lady Anne, it is wonderful to see you," Elizabeth said, pulling back from the embrace. "What a lovely surprise. I was under the impression you had already left this part of the country for London."

"Oh, no! I could not have left Hertfordshire without seeing you. I apologize for my delayed visit."

"You came, and I cannot express what it means

to me. I am certain my father will regret missing you."

"I believe your father and my husband had a very pleasant visit."

Elizabeth nodded. "I believe they did."

After conversing for a few minutes while tea was being served, Lady Anne seized the opportunity of the servant's departure to get to the point of her visit. "Elizabeth, I must speak with you about something very important," she said.

Lady Anne took a deep breath before continuing. "My dear, I fear I have willfully misunderstood the feelings between you and my son. I know now that I was wrong to try to keep you two apart."

Elizabeth's heart leaped with hope at Lady Anne's words. Could it be possible that Lady Anne had come to accept her as a suitable match for her son?

Lady Anne confessed to Elizabeth that she had been a selfish woman her entire life, never more so than when she put her own interests above those of her most-beloved son.

"Because of my stance, you have suffered too much, and I aim to make amends."

"I understand you were doing what you felt was best. How can I not be grateful to you for providing me with such a wonderful upbringing and shaping me into the person I am? What do I not owe you?"

"Elizabeth, there is something that has been weighing on my heart for years, something I have never shared with anyone. Yes, I did raise you as though you were my own daughter, and I have loved every moment of it. Yet, I have also agonized in silence over the means it was brought about.

"I am not so foolish as to believe that had it not been for me, your mother might still be alive, but I cannot help but feel that my words contributed to your family's abrupt departure from Pemberley. For the longest time, it seemed as though my holding fast to my conviction was my way of shielding myself against culpability for what had transpired.

"You see, your mother and I exchanged harsh words that, despite representing my firm beliefs at the time, might have been better left unsaid."

All the while Lady Anne spoke Elizabeth remained silent, which was sufficient encouragement for the older woman to continue.

"Your mother entertained the idea of a union between one of her daughters and Fitzwilliam.

Knowing my opinion on the subject, you can surely imagine the indelicacy of my response.

"I say all this to express how sorry I am to have belittled your mother's fondest wish for her offspring—quite possibly one of her final wishes—and I am still sorry for continuing to prevent its realization.

"I suppose I could have told you this sooner, but I feared you would resent me for wounding your mother's feelings. Now that I have told you, do you think you will ever see me the same way? Do you hate me for what I did?"

Setting her teacup aside, Elizabeth took Lady Anne's hand in hers. "I could never hate you, and I certainly do not blame you for what may have happened in the past. I cannot fathom the impact your stance may have had on my mother, but I am certain it would not have altered her fate."

"Dearest Elizabeth, your understanding is truly more than I deserve," cried Lady Anne. "I wish I could say that was my only cause for regret, but there is more. Indeed, I can barely countenance the version of myself that resorted to such intrusive means to keep you and my son apart. You must know by now that I intercepted your parting letter to my son on the day you left Pemberley. I stood by and witnessed firsthand my own son's heartbreak over the belief that you had left without saying goodbye—all to fulfill my own selfish desires."

Here, she released her ladyship's hand. Her voice tentative, Elizabeth said, "I confess when I first realized what had happened that I was upset with you for keeping my letter from Fitzwilliam. However, its sting has long since faded."

"My child, you have never been one to cling to old grievances. Despite my desire to believe that what you felt for Fitzwilliam was akin to infatuation, I was wrong to adhere to such a notion rather than admit what was so plain to see. I know how much you and Fitzwilliam love each other. I may not be able to take back the things I said to your mother, but I can certainly make amends by letting go of my preconceived notions and allowing her wish to unfold." Her ladyship recaptured Elizabeth's hands in hers.

"Fitzwilliam told me that you will not accept his proposal without my blessing. Well, I am happy to say that you have it, my dear. And I will tell you, just as I told him during our long overdue talk, that you deserve each other's love. I could not have parted with you to anyone less worthy."

Elizabeth's reaction upon receiving Lady Anne's blessing was everything one could expect. Her heart soared with joy. After lingering in doubt for so long, she never expected Lady Anne to embrace the idea of having her as a daughter-in-law.

"Thank you, Lady Anne," she said, tears pricking at the corners of her eyes. "I cannot express how much this means to me."

"I only wish that I had realized sooner how important you are to my son. Please forgive me."

Elizabeth's busy mind was in a whirl. Perhaps she was being far too generous toward Lady Anne, but knowing the wait was nearly over for her and Fitzwilliam was all that she could think of—that and her personal philosophy to think only of the past as its remembrance brought her pleasure.

"Yes!" Elizabeth said, smiling through her tears. "Yes, I forgive you a thousand times over."

Fitzwilliam's conversation with his mother had given him hope that, finally, his happiness was soon to be guaranteed, so much so that he arrived at Longbourn not a good half-hour after his parents set off for London.

Their visit had barely begun when Fitzwilliam asked, "Shall we take a turn outside, Elizabeth?"

Elizabeth's eyes twinkled with delight as she accepted his offer. She led him to the garden, a secluded haven of vibrant blooms and winding paths.

The scent of flowers perfumed the air as they strolled hand in hand, the late afternoon sun casting a golden glow on their faces. Their laughter mingled with the chirping of birds, creating a symphony of blissful melodies. The garden seemed to conspire with them, crafting an intimate atmosphere that mirrored the couple's boundless love.

Finally finding themselves in a secluded arbor draped with climbing ivy, they turned to face each other. Fitzwilliam's heart raced as he took a deep breath, the significance of his intentions weighing heavy on his chest.

With all the grace befitting a gentleman, he dropped down on one knee, his eyes fixed on hers. "Elizabeth, my love, I cannot bear to wait a moment longer. Will you honor me by becoming my wife?"

. . .

Elizabeth's breath caught in her throat as she beheld the man who had captured her heart so long ago. A mix of emotions swirled within her—joy, love, and an overwhelming sense of belonging. She nodded, her countenance beaming with happiness. "Yes, Fitzwilliam, I will be your wife."

Time stood still as Fitzwilliam stood and retrieved a ring from his pocket. He held Elizabeth's hand, his touch sending shivers of anticipation up her arm. As he delicately placed the dazzling ring on her finger, he said, "My mother wishes for you to have this, my love. It belonged to her, given to her by her mother, the former Countess of Matlock."

Elizabeth's eyes widened in recognition as she looked at the exquisite piece of jewelry adorning her finger. She knew the ring well, having seen Lady Anne wearing it on many significant occasions throughout the years, including Elizabeth's coming-out ball—it was a cherished family heirloom indeed. Lady Anne had often spoken of its significance.

A rush of emotion overwhelmed her as she realized the depth of Lady Anne's acceptance.

Tears welled up in her eyes as she looked at Fitzwilliam, her voice choked with gratitude. "Oh, Fitzwilliam, this ring... I know its history. Lady Anne had intended for it to be given to her daughter." She pressed her palm to her bosom. "And now she has given it to me."

Fitzwilliam's eyes shimmered with unshed tears as he cupped Elizabeth's face in his hands. "She has always loved you as her own, Elizabeth. And now that you are to be my wife, no doubt her love for you has grown."

With the history of their past and the promise of their future entwined, Fitzwilliam and Elizabeth sealed their engagement with a kiss—a kiss that spoke of boundless love and a long list of shared adventures. The world around them seemed to fade into insignificance as they lost themselves in their tender embrace, their hearts beating as one.

At length, they pulled away, their foreheads resting against each other's. Fitzwilliam said, "You have made me the happiest man alive, Elizabeth."

"Oh, Fitzwilliam, being with you fulfills my every fantasy of what a love of a lifetime ought to be," Elizabeth replied, her voice filled with awe.

He gently pressed his lips against hers, a

tender caress that hinted of long unspoken yearnings. "My dearest, loveliest Elizabeth," he uttered, his voice a melodic whisper that echoed in her heart. "You have seen nothing yet. What lies ahead for us is beyond your wildest dreams."

Epilogue

THE DAY of the wedding was one of unadulterated joy and celebration. As Elizabeth, radiant in her gown of soft white silk, stepped onto her father's arm, Mr. Bennet felt his heart swell with pride unlike anything he had ever suffered. His Lizzy was getting married—to the love of her life no less—and nothing could eclipse the happiness he felt for her.

The ceremony was a beautiful blur of laughter and happy tears, culminating in jubilant applause that echoed through the church as Fitzwilliam and Elizabeth sealed their union with a kiss. That day, as he watched them leave the church, a married couple bound by love, he knew he was witnessing a tale that would be spoken of for generations to come.

Even more joyful was the fact that although she would one day reside in Derbyshire as the mistress of Pemberley, for now she was only three short miles away. The newlyweds had decided to reside in Netherfield Park, choosing the intimacy and tranquility of the smaller estate over the grandeur of Pemberley. Despite the Netherfield library not having the same splendor as the one at Pemberley, it was a small sacrifice for the joy that his daughter's nearness brought. The happiness in Elizabeth's eyes and her beaming smile as she navigated her role as the mistress of Netherfield was worth more than all the tomes in Derbyshire.

As for others' reactions to the marriage, they were diverse and numerous. Elizabeth's aunt Phillips, whose lack of sense and sensibility proved a great trial during her brief period of courtship, became too much in awe in Fitzwilliam's presence to be really vulgar. Aside from the blessings of her father, Mr. Darcy, and Lady Anne, Elizabeth considered the Gardiners' approval the greatest source of satisfaction. When they all spent Christmas in Hertfordshire, Fitzwilliam's affection for them progressed from liking to loving in no time at all, as did the Gardiners' sentiments toward him.

If only the same could be said of Fitzwilliam's feelings for his wife's other relative, Mr. William Collins. The latter had finally met Fitzwilliam at his and Charlotte's own wedding breakfast. It was then that Collins comprehended the reason behind his cousin Elizabeth's refusal of his marriage proposal. She was not imprudent, as he had taught himself to believe. On the contrary, his cousin was clever. She had been biding her time in the hope of a far larger catch, and what a catch indeed. To boast of a familial acquaintance with someone like Fitzwilliam Darcy was really something, in Collins' opinion. It held equal, if not greater, weight than his pride in his noble patroness, Lady Catherine de Bourgh. Upon reflection, he had to concede that in terms of his newly elevated standing, the outcome had been far better than he'd had any reason to hope for.

Elizabeth kept up a steady correspondence with Charlotte. She cherished their friendship and wished to return the courtesy of the lengthy visits that Charlotte always extended to her when she was in Hertfordshire. However, Charlotte's residence in Kent under the patronage of Lady

Catherine de Bourgh gave Elizabeth considerable pause and something to think of.

Outrage barely covered what Lady Catherine felt upon hearing the news of her nephew's impending wedding to Elizabeth Bennet. She had not been shy about expressing her objections about the young lady, whose upbringing had encouraged her to reach for a station in life she did not deserve, and she held fast to her opinion with vigor.

The sight of her beloved mother's ring on Elizabeth's finger—a ring that should have been passed on to Anne—was the source of enduring anger and considerable vexation. The fury was more pronounced given that it was her sister doing. The idea of a Bennet marrying into the esteemed Fitzwilliam family was an affront to her, something that she had always looked upon with scorn. The matter of her sister, Lady Anne, sanctioning the sordid affair was another blow to her sensibility.

Lady Catherine was of the firm belief that Elizabeth would never do anything to displease Lady Anne, and she had allowed herself to depend on it. The idea of her sister encouraging Fitzwilliam and Elizabeth to follow their hearts was a betrayal that Lady Catherine found hard to swallow. And while Elizabeth and Fitzwilliam went about their happy lives, regardless of her discontent, Lady Catherine seethed in the confines of Rosings Park, nursing her wounded pride, all the while blaming Lady Anne, who, against all odds and expectations, had given her blessings on the union and, in so doing, had been the means of uniting them.

Obstinate! Headstrong girl! These were the words Lady Catherine used to describe her nephew's bride. Elizabeth, however, wore this characterization as a badge of honor. She was proud of her spirit, her courage, and the steadfast commitment she held for Fitzwilliam. Even during those moments when all hope seemed in vain, she never wavered in her love for him. She measured every man she had ever met against him, and in every instance she found the other man wanting. Indeed, it was true she had not met all that many men in her life. She was very much a proponent of probabilities, more so than possibilities. While it was certainly possible that she might have met someone whom she deemed more worthy than Fitzwilliam Darcy, she did not think it was very probable, for in Elizabeth's opinion, Fitzwilliam had always been and always would be the best man in the world.

And so, together as one, they embarked on a future that sparkled with promise and conviction, their love forever woven in the tapestry of their shared lives—a love that, in its purest form, was nothing short of simply beautiful.

The End

Also by P. O. Dixon

Standalone

Simply Beautiful

Her Spirits Rising to Playfulness

Mr. Darcy, the Heir of Pemberley

Abounds with Gaieties

After Last Night with Mr. Darcy

Somebody Else's Gentleman

Something to Think Of

Wait for Love

Most Ardently, Most Unknowingly in Love

A Favorite Daughter

Gravity

Expecting His Wife

The Means of Uniting Them

Designed for Each Other

Together in Perfect Felicity

Which that Season Brings

Christmas Sealed with a Kiss

Christmas, Love and Mr. Darcy

A Night with Mr. Darcy to Remember

By Reason, by Reflection, by Everything

Impertinent Strangers

Bewitched, Body and Soul

To Refuse Such a Man

Miss Elizabeth Bennet

Still a Young Man

Love Will Grow

Only a Heartbeat Away

As Good as a Lord

Matter of Trust

Expecting His Proposal

Pride and Sensuality

A Tender Moment

Almost Persuaded

Series

Everything Will Change

Lady Elizabeth

So Far Away

Dearest, Loveliest Elizabeth

Dearest Elizabeth

Loveliest Elizabeth

Dearest, Loveliest Elizabeth

A Darcy and Elizabeth Love Affair

A Lasting Love Affair

'Tis the Season for Matchmaking

Pride and Prejudice Untold

To Have His Cake (and Eat it Too)

What He Would Not Do

Lady Harriette

Darcy and the Young Knight's Quest

He Taught Me to Hope

The Mission

Hope and Sensibility

Visit http://podixon.com for more.

About the Author

P. O. Dixon is a writer as well as an entertainer. Historical England and its days of yore fascinate her. She, in particular, loves the Regency period with its strict mores and oh so proper decorum. Her ardent appreciation of Jane Austen's timeless works set her on the writer's journey—swapping boardrooms for ballrooms and never looking back.

Connect with the Author

Website: podixon.com
YouTube: https://www.youtube.com/@PODIXONAUDIOBOOKS
Newsletter: bit.ly/SuchHappyNews
Email: podixon@podixon.com
Twitter: @podixon
Facebook: facebook.com/podixon